NURSING REVISION NOTES

EAR NOSE AND THROAT NURSING

NURSING REVISION NOTES

EAR NOSE AND THROAT NURSING

By
S. A. Garlick SRN; DN; SCM; Cert. Ed.

CELTIC
REVISION AIDS

Celtic Revision Aids

30–32 Gray's Inn Road
London WC1X 8JL

First Published 1984

Printed and bound in Great Britain by
Cox & Wyman Ltd, Reading

GENERAL EDITOR'S FOREWORD

The nursing revision series is designed for all nurses in training. The notes are suitable for pre-modular study, post-modular revision and examination revision, and will also be of value to learners undertaking ongoing assessment. While being comprehensive in the major areas of both patient condition and nursing care, they are intended to complement, not replace, existing text books. Each book provides information on basic anatomy and physiology, aspects of investigations and nursing care and practice questions and answers are included at the end of each section. The authors have used their experience in nurse education to select important areas of nursing care for inclusion and I am sure that all nurse learners will find the books of continuing value throughout their training.

P.J. Morland
Lecturer
Department of Education
University College Cardiff

AUTHOR'S FOREWORD

These notes are intended for nurses who are studying the subject of E.N.T. in study block/module, revising for examinations and working within the E.N.T. area.

It is hoped they will help learners to understand some of the more common conditions within this speciality and in doing so help them to be able to identify patients' problems and so be able to plan and give appropriate care. This care will, of course, vary according to local practice.

CONTENTS

1 STRUCTURE AND FUNCTIONS OF THE EAR

The objectives of this section are to:

1. Describe briefly the structure and function of the ear;
2. Explain the more common conditions which may affect the ear, the patient's treatment and their nursing care;
3. Identify some of the problems of adults and children with a hearing loss;
4. Outline the help available for adults and children with hearing problems.

The ear

The ear is the organ of hearing and is also concerned with balance.

It is situated in the temporal bone of the skull and may be divided into three parts, the external, middle and inner part.

External ear

This is made up of two parts: the pinna or auricle and the external auditory meatus.

Pinna

The pina develops in the embryo from six tubercules which then fuse together.

It is irregular in shape and formed from yellow elastic cartilage with some fatty tissue in the lobe. The pinna is covered by skin which is closely bound down to the perichondrium of the cartilage. Animals have the ability to move the pinna but this is now almost lost in man.

External auditory meatus

This is an S shaped canal about 2.5 cm (1 inch) in length the outer third being cartilage the inner two thirds bone. The canal is lined by skin which has the special property of lateral migration which provides a self-cleaning mechanism. In the cartilaginous part of the meatus can be seen hair follicles, sebaceous and ceruminous glands. It is the secretions of these glands which form wax.

The direction of the meatus is upwards, backwards, then downwards and forwards. This means in adults the pinna must be pulled upwards and backwards to straighten the canal when examining the ear. In the child the meatus is shorter and straighter.

At the medial end of the meatus is the tympanic membrane. It is set at an angle so that the floor and the anterior wall of the meatus are longer than the roof and posterior wall.

Tympanic membrane

The tympanic membrane or eardrum separates the external ear from the middle ear. It is a thin pearly grey mobile sheet made up of three layers, squamous epithelium, fibrous tissue and mucous membrane. The squamous epithelium is continuous with the lining of the meatus, while the mucous membrane is the lining of the middle ear. Embedded in the middle fibrous layer is the long process or handle of the malleus. This fibrous layer is deficient in the upper part of the drum. A conical shaped light reflex can be seen projected from the handle of the malleus to the drum margin. This is produced by the angle of the drum.

Middle ear

The middle ear cleft is a collective term used to describe the tympanic cavity, the Eustachian tube and the mastoid antrum, and air cells. Continuous mucous membrane lines all the structures.

The middle ear or tympanic cavity is an air-conditioning space in the middle ear which communicates with the naso pharynx by means of the Eustachian tube, and the mastoid air cells by means of the aditus ad antrum.

Eustachian tube

This is a boney and cartilaginous tube about 1½ inches in length which passes from the anterior wall of the middle ear downwards and forwards to the naso pharynx. It is opened during swallowing and yawning by the action of the pharyngeal muscles. The function of the Eustachian tube is to aeriate the middle ear and to equalise the pressure between the middle ear and the external meatus. This is essential for normal hearing.

Mastoid antrum and air cells

The mastoid antrum is a space behind the middle ear. It communicates with the middle ear by means of a small opening, the aditus, and with the mastoid air cells behind. These mastoid cells vary in number and may be absent or extensively distributed throughout the mastoid process. The degree of pneumatization of the mastoid will depend on aeriation during development in childhood.

Structures within the Middle Ear Cavity

The ossicles

Three small bones the malleus, incus and stapes cross the middle ear articulating with each other. The long process of the malleus lies within the drum while the foot plate of the stapes occupies the oval window of the inner ear (See Fig 1).

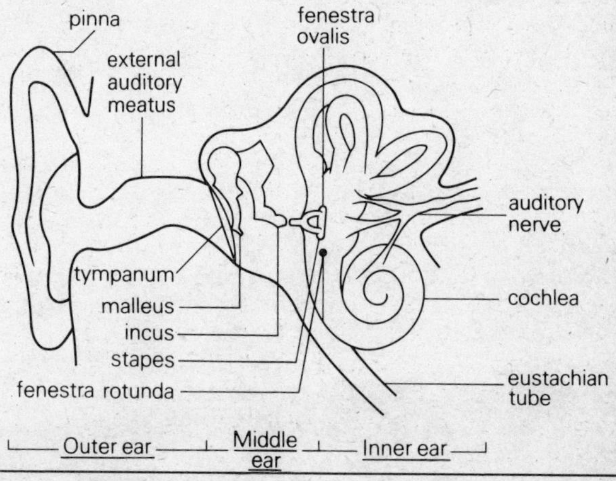

The ear

Fig 1

Tensa tympani and Stapedius
These are two muscles within the middle ear. They restrict movement of the drum and ossicles in the presence of loud noise, and so protect against noise trauma.

Corda tympani
A branch of the facial nerve, the corda tympani crosses the middle ear and supplies the anterior part of the tongue with the sensation of taste.

Relationships
Some of the important structures which are related to the middle ear are:

Superior — middle cranial fossa
Inferior — Jugular bulb, cranial nerves ix, x, xi
Anterior — Eustachian tube
Posterior — Aditus ad antrum leading to the mastoid air cells
Medially — Inner ear

The inner ear structures which can be seen on the medial wall of the inner ear are the promontory, lateral semi-circular canal and the oval and round windows.

Running in a bony canal and closely related to the middle ear is the facial nerve.

Fig 2 Membranous labyrinth

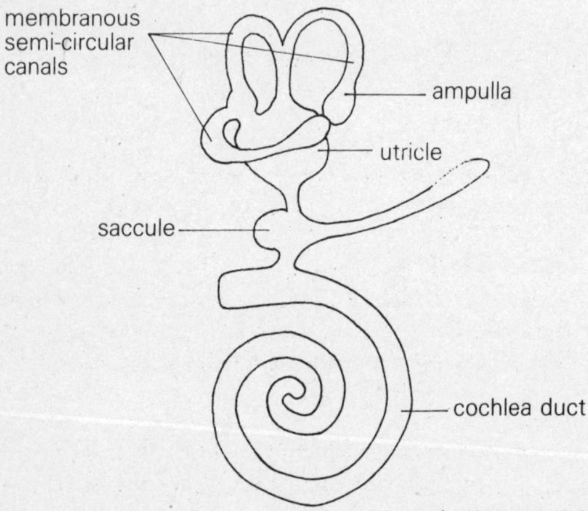

Fig 3 Cross section of cochlea

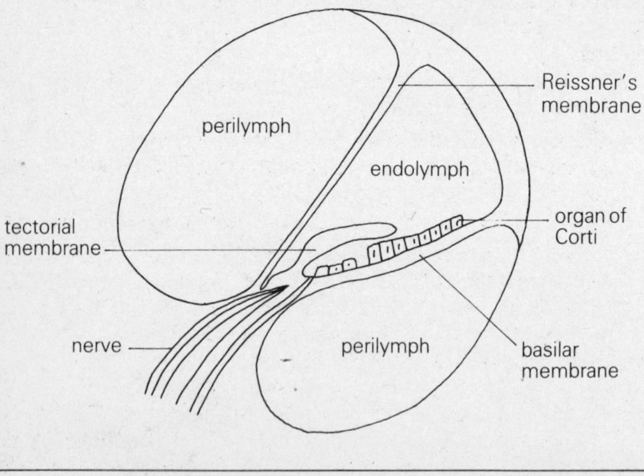

Inner ear

The inner ear is made up of a hard bony shell called the bony labyrinth containing a fluid called perilymph, within which is suspended the delicate membranous labyrinth.

Bony labyrinth

This is a series of canals made up of three parts, the cochlea, the vestibule and the semi-circular canals.

Cochlea

The cochlea is a hollow spiral tube resembling a snail shell which opens into the vestibule. Its basal part forms the promontory of the inner ear.

Vestibule

This lies between the cochlea and the semi-circular canals and is perforated by the oval and round windows. These windows are covered by the stapes foot plate and the round window membrane respectively.

Semi-circular canals

There are three semi-circular canals: the superior, lateral or horizontal, and the posterior, set at right angles to each other in the three planes of space. Each has an enlargement at one end called the ampulla.

Membranous labyrinth

Suspended within the bony labyrinth protected by it and having a similar shape is the membranous labyrinth. This is made up of a series of canals and sacs containing the fluid endolymph.

Cochlea Duct

The bony cochlea is divided into three canals along its length by the basilar and Reissner membranes.

The central canal is the membranous cochlea or cochlea duct. It is triangular in shape and contains endolymph. The two outer canals contain perilymph. These canals join together at the apex of the cochlea while the oposite ends are closed by the oval and round windows.

Situated on the basilar membrane and running the whole length of the cochlea duct is the Organ of Corti. This is made up of highly specialised neuro-epithelial tissue with hair cells. The nerve fibres of the cochlea part of the auditory nerve commence at the Organ of Corti. Suspended above it is the tectorial membrane.

Each frequency of sound has its place on the Organ of Corti.

Membranous semi-circular canals

There are three membranous semi-circular canals containing endolymph lying within the bony semi-circular canals. One end of each is dilated to form an ampulla containing the end organs of balance called crista. The crista is made up of special neuro-epithelium with hairs embedded in a gelatinous substance called cupula. Movement of the endolymph causes displacement of the cupula and hair cells stimulating the nerve endings. The crista is therefore stimulated by movement of the head.

Utricle and saccule

These are two membranous sacs containing endolymph which are situated within the vestibule. They lie between the cochlea duct and the membranous semi-circular canals and are linked to them by ducts. The utricle contains specialised neuro-epithelium called macula which is similar to the crista except that the overlying substance contains particles of calcium carbonate, called otoliths. The utricle is concerned with the position of the head in space, while the function of the saccule is unknown.

Nerve endings from the crista and macula form the two vestibular branches of the auditory nerve.

Auditory nerve

The auditory nerve is the eighth cranial nerve and is formed by the cochlea and vestibular branches which are concerned with hearing and balance. Leaving the ear in a bony canal called the internal auditory meatus the nerve passes through various relay stations to the brain.

Hearing

Sound may be conducted to the cochlea via the external and middle ear, that is by air conduction, or by bone conduction directly through the bones of the skull.

Sound waves are collected by the pinna, pass down the external auditory meatus — causing the ear drum to vibrate. Due to the fact that the handle of the malleus is attached to the drum the movement will be transmitted across the middle ear through the malleus and incus to the stapes.

The stapes will move with a rocking tilting movement in the oval window causing a disturbance of the perilymph in the cochlea. This will be transmitted through the perilymph causing what is known as the 'round window reflex' when the round window bulges in opposition to the stapes movement. Therefore there should always be preferential distribution of sound to one window so that this reflex action can occur.

The movement of the perilymph in the bony canal will cause undulation of the cochlea duct. This wave of movement will be at its maximum when it reaches the place on the Organ of Corti corresponding to the frequency of the sound. It will then die away. High frequency sounds are processed at the basal part of the cochlea, low on the apex.

Movement of the cochlea duct will cause movement of the endolymph. As the basilar membrane moves the hair cell of the Organ of Corti will have a shearing movement against the tectorial membrane. At this point physical energy is converted in some way into electrical energy and the nerve endings are stimulated. Nerve impulses are carried via the cochlea part of the auditory nerve to the auditory centres in the brain.

Sound which is heard by bone conduction is transmitted through the bones of the skull to the cochlea.

The physiology of how we hear is still not fully understood.

Sound

Sound is produced by a moving vibrating source and must have a medium such as air or fluid to travel through.

The sound waves are made up of cycles of compression and rarefaction of the molecules of the media through which they travel.

The frequency of a sound is the number of cycles which takes place in 1 second and is expressed as Hertz (Hz).

The pitch of a sound is determined by the frequency. The greater the frequency the higher the pitch perceived.

Amplitude or loudness is measured in decibels (dB).

Vestibular function

The function of the vestibular part of the ear is, in conjunction with the eyes and propreceptors, to control the position and movement of the body in space.

The utricle is concerned with position in space in the vertical plane. It relates to gravity and linear acceleration which is the movement such as is experienced in a lift. When the head is horizontal and straight the macula is quiescent but will respond to the slightest tilting.

The semi-circular canals respond to active movement, such as rotation, progression in a straight line, or acceleration.

Any movement of the head will cause movement of the endolymph and displacement of the macula and crista. The hair processes are bent, the hair cell stimulated and impulses are carried via the vestibular part of the auditory nerve to the brain. Over stimulation of the labyrinth will cause giddiness.

Practice questions

Structure and functions of the ear

1. Explain briefly the function of the:
   a Eustachian tube
   b Cordi tympani
   c Tensa tympani
   d Ossicles
   e Round window reflex
2. Relate the following structures to their anatomical position around the middle ear:
   a Aditus ad antrum
   b Eustachian tube
   c Promentory
   d Jugular bulb
   e Vagus nerve
   f Middle cranial fossa
   g Lateral semi-circular canal
   h Tympanic membrane

Fill in the blank spaces.

3. The .... of the stapes is situated in the .... window.
4. Surrounding the cochlea duct is the fluid ....
5. .... is the fluid within the bony ampulla.
6. The fluid within the saccule is ....
7. Sound waves must have a .... to travel through.
8. Frequency of sound is measured in ....
9. .... of sound is determined by frequency.
10. Loudness of sound is measured in ....
11. The pinna of the ear in the embryo is formed from ....
12. The skin of the external meatus has the property of ....
13. When examining the ear the pinna must be pulled ....
14. The outer third of the meatus has ....
15. Describe briefly how we hear.
16. Cordi tympani is a:
    a Muscle
    b Nerve
    c Ligament
    d Part of the ear drum
17. Movement such as going up in a lift will stimulate the:
    a Utricle
    b Saccule
    c Semi-circular canals
    d Organ of Corti

18. The Organ of Corti is situated on the:
    a Reissner's membrane
    b Tectoral membrane
    c Round window membrane
    d Basilar membrane
19. Rotation of the head will stimulate the:
    a Crista
    b Macula
    c Ampulla
    d Otolith
20. Which cranial nerve is closely related anatomically to the middle ear and may be involved in middle ear disease?
    a 7th cranial nerve
    b 8th cranial nerve
    c 5th cranial nerve
    d 3rd cranial nerve
21. The lateral layer of the tympanic membrane is:
    a Mucous membrane
    b Fibrous tissue
    c Columnar epithelium
    d Squamous epithelium
22. A normal ear drum will look:
    a Pink
    b Blue
    c Grey
    d Yellow
23. Which of the following statements relate to the Eustachian tube?
    a It passes from the middle ear to the oral pharynx.
    b Its length is about 2.5 cm.
    c It is composed of cartilage.
    d It passes from the middle ear to the naso pharynx.

Answers

1. **a** Eustachian tube — to aeriate the middle ear and equalise the pressure on both sides of the drum.
   b Cordi tympani is a branch of the facial nerve supplying the anterior part of the tongue with taste.
   c The tensa tympani with the stapedius muscle prevents too much movement of the drum ossicles in the presence of a loud noise and so protect the inner ear.
   d Sound is transmitted across the middle ear by the movement of the malleus, incus and stapes — the ossicles.

e Round window reflex — is the movement of the round window membrane in opposition to the movement of the stapes and necessary for normal hearing.

2. **a** Posterior
   b Anterior
   c Medial
   d Inferior
   e Inferior
   f Superior
   g Medial
   h Lateral
3. Footplate — oval.
4. Perilymph.
5. Perilymph.
6. Endolymph.
7. Medium.
8. Hz.
9. Pitch.
10. dB.
11. 6 tubercules.
12. Lateral migration.
13. Upwards and backwards.
14. Hair follicles, sebaceous glands, ceruminous glands.
15. Sound waves are picked up by the pinna
    — pass down the meatus
    — vibration of the tympanic membrane
    — movement of malleus, incus, stapes
    — movment of stapes footplate in oval window
    — movement of perilymph
    — waves passing along cochlea duct
    — movement of perilymph
    — shearing movement of hair cells of Organ of Corti and tectoral membrane
    — nerve endings stimulated
    — impulse passes along the cochlea branch of the auditory nerve to the brain.
16. **b**
17. **a**
18. **d**
19. **a**
20. **a**
21. **d**
22. **c**
23. **d**

2 CONDITIONS OF THE EAR AND EXAMINATION TESTS

Patients presenting to the ENT department with diseases of the ear will be complaining of one or more of the following problems.

Otalgia
Otalgia or earache may occur as a symptom of ear disease or may be referred pain from the throat or teeth.

Otorrhoea
Discharge from the ear can be serous, mucoid, purulent, blood stained and at times offensive.

Deafness
The inability to hear may vary from a slight hearing loss to almost total deafness. Deafness may be of two types:

Conductive — which may be caused by anything which prevents sound reaching the inner ear.

Sensori-neural— this may involve the cochlea, auditory nerve, auditory pathways or centre in the brain.

Vertigo
Vertigo or giddiness is experiencing movement which is not present, and indicates a disturbance of the balance mechanism of the ear.

Tinnitus
Tinnitus is the sensation of noises in the ear or the head. Usually associated with inner ear conditions rather than middle or outer.

Any of these symptoms, however, may arise from conditions outside the ear.

Examination of the ear

The pinna is examined, any abnormality of shape is noted, also the condition of the skin. Post aurally signs of swelling and tenderness over the mastoid process are looked for.

An aural speculum is used to examine the meatus and drum, the pinna being pulled upwards and backwards to straighten the canal. It may be necessary to remove any wax. Mobility of the drum is demonstrated by using a Siegle's speculum.

Hearing can be tested by whispered voice, tuning fork tests and audiometry.

Whispered voice
The examiner whispers words at various distances from the patient which they should then repeat.

Tuning fork tests
The two tests generally done are the Rinne and Weber. A 512 tuning fork is commonly used.

Rinne test
This differenciates between conductive and sensori neural deafness by comparing air and bone conduction.

A vibrating tuning fork is held near to the meatus and put onto the mastoid process. The patient's ability to hear the two is compared. Normally the air conduction is better than the bone conduction.
This is known as Rinne positive. With a conductive deafness the sound is heard better when the tuning fork is on the mastoid process and is then regarded as Rinne negative.

Weber Test
A tuning fork placed in the centre of the head will normally be heard equally in both ears. With a conductive deafness in one ear the sound will be lateralized to the deaf ear because that ear is not picking up ambient sound. In sensori neural deafness the sound is heard best in the good ear.

Audiometry
An audiometer is a machine which produces pure tones at different frequencies ranging from 250–8000 Hz. Each frequency can be presented at different intensities going up in 5–10 dB steps. A pure tone is delivered to each ear in turn, the intensity being increased until the sound is just heard. This is known as the threshold for that frequency.

Speech audiometry may be undertaken. Phonetically balanced words are put into each ear at different frequencies and the result charted on a line graph.
Hearing may also be tested by more sophisticated objective forms of audiometer. One of these is now commonly used in impedance audiometry. This measures the impedance of the drum by putting sound into the meatus and measuring the amount reflected.

Vestibular function tests

Vestibular function may be assessed by various tests the one being most used is the caloric test. In these tests nystagmus, which is involuntary rapid to and fro eye movements, is stimulated.

Caloric Test

The patient lies with their head at an angle of 30° which brings the lateral semi-circular canal into the vertical plane. Each ear is in turn irrigated with water 7° above and below body temperature (30°C 44°C) for 40 seconds. Nystagmus will be stimulated and normally lasts about 2 minutes. The time between the beginning of the irrigation and the end of the nystagmus is recorded. If the time is reduced in both the hot and cold test in one ear it is said there is a canal paresis on that side.

Electronystagmography

This is a means of recording the eye movements during vestibular function tests. Electrodes are placed on the skin near to the eyes and connected to the machine. Impulses are picked up, amplified and recorded on a write out. This is more exact than observation of nystagmus which is not always easy to see.

(ii) Conditions of the external ear

The external ear may be affected by congenital abnormalities, trauma, foreign bodies or inflammatory conditions.

Conditions of the Pinna

Congenital

The pinna develops from six tubercules and various defects may arise from malfusion. A baby may be born with any abnormality ranging from a complete absence of pinna to an extra one. Probably the most common abnormality of shape is that of 'bat ear'.

Treatment

It may be decided to do nothing and let the hair cover the defect, or surgery is undertaken. Surgery can range from removal of the extra appendage to reconstructing a new pinna; or whatever is necessary to alter the shape. Bat ears may be corrected by the operation of otoplasty.

Haematoma

Trauma to the ear is usually seen in young men and is associated with such pursuits as fighting, boxing and other sports. A blow to the ear can cause bleeding between the cartilage and perichondrium with haematoma formation. Elevation of the perichondrium by the haemotoma will cut off the blood supply to the cartilage resulting in necrosis. This can then cause scarring, fibrosis and the so called 'cauliflower ear'.

Treatment

This is aspiration or incision of the haematoma and the application of a firm bandage. Antibiotics may be given prophylactically. Should the haematoma become infected an abscess can form.

Pericondritis

Pericondritis is infection of the pinna and may be secondary to a haematoma or as a complication of surgery when the incision has become infected.

Treatment

Antibiotics will be given and any abscess incised and drained. Deformity of the pinna can result in a cauliflower ear.

Skin conditions

The skin of the pinna may be affected by any of the usual skin conditions such as eczema. An extension of the external otitis of the meatus may cause the pinna to become red, swollen, cracked, weeping and painful. The topical treatment given will depend on the cause.

Conditions of the external auditory meatus

The external middle and inner ear develop separately in the embryo and later join together. Congenital abnormalities of one part may occur while the rest of the ear may be normal, or defects can affect all three.

Meatal atresia

When a child is born with a meatal atresia investigation must be carried out to assess the development of the middle and inner ear and also the condition of the other ear. Should the abnormality be unilateral and the second ear normal, treatment will probably be left until the child is older. When both ears are affected every effort must be made to get sound to the inner ear so that speech may develop naturally.

A meatoplasty which is the formation of a new canal may be undertaken and a tympanic membrane is also constructed. Even when the middle or inner ear are found to be abnormal a new meatus can be made to accommodate a hearing aid mould.

Foreign bodies

Some children have a great tendency to put small objects such as paper, beads or seeds into the ear. These may remain unnoticed or they may produce inflammation, pain and deafness if the meatus is blocked.

Treatment

This is removal, using a good light and the proper instruments. Some objects may be picked out with forceps, or sucked out. However, round objects must be removed by passing a small blunt hook behind them. It is essential that the child is quiet and still, which could mean giving a general anaesthetic.

Some foreign bodies can be removed by syringing but not things such as peas which would swell. Should an insect fly into the meatus it can be killed by instilling a little warm vegetable oil and then syringed out.

The potential dangers of a foreign body in the ear are trauma to the meatal wall or the drum, risk of the foreign body being pushed through the drum and damaging the middle ear structures. Trauma may also be caused by unskilled removal.

Wax

Wax is formed by the secretions of the glands in the outer part of the meatus and should normally migrate out of the canal. However in some individuals wax may either be produced in large quantities, be hard in consistency or fail to be extruded from the canal. This can then form a hard mass which blocks the meatus causing deafness and possibly pain and irritation.

Wax can be removed either by using instruments, suction or by syringing. Syringing an ear is a procedure which is generally carried out by trained nurses. It is not without risk of trauma to the ear and so should be done after instruction and with supervision until competent.

The principles of the procedure of syringing an ear are as follows.

a There should be no evidence of a perforation of the drum.

b The fluid being used must be at body temperature or the patient will feel giddy.

c The stream of fluid must be directed along the posterior superior meatal wall.

d After the wax is removed the ear must be examined for any signs of trauma.

e The meatus must be mopped dry.

Hard wax should be softened by instilling drops such as warm olive oil or soda bicarbonate for a few days prior to syringing. Proprietary wax softners may in some instances cause otitis externa.

Furunculosis

A furuncule or boil is a staphylococcal infection of a hair follicle and so occurs in the outer part of the meatus. The patient complains of irritation and pain, particularly when the ear is examined or when the pinna is moved. There may be trismus, possibly an enlarged lymph gland and deafness if the meatus is blocked.

Treatment

Antibiotics are usually given and a half inch ribbon gauze wick soaked in a solution like glycerine and ichthammol is put into the meatus. This is changed regularly until the furuncule bursts and then aurul toilet will be carried out to remove the discharge. Analgesics are given for pain.

Furunculosis tends to occur in diabetics so patients who report with this condition recurring should have their urine tested.

External otitis

External otitis is an inflammatory condition of the skin of the external auditory meatus which may also involve the pinna. It is a condition to which some people are more susceptible than others. Possible causes are many and may be interrelated. Water and moisture in the meatus is always a pre-disposing factor. It can be caused by any of the following.

Allergy

The allergic response may be to irritants such as hair sprays, nickel in earrings or wax softening solutions. Antibiotic ear drops, for example penicillin, which may originally be prescribed for the condition, probably by the G.P., may actually exacerbate it.

Trauma

This may commonly be caused by scratching or poking down the ear, or possibly by the presence of a foreign body.

Bacterial infection

This may be caused by organisms such as staphyloccus aureus, streptococcus, or pseudomonas pyocyaneus. Organisms may gain access following trauma.

Fungal infection

A fungal infection may be primary or secondary to a bacterial infection. It can occur as a result of the topical use of antibiotics. The common fungi being aspergillus niger and candida albicans.

Skin conditions

External otitis can be a continuation of skin conditions such as eczema or dandruff.

Wax

External otitis can be caused either by the irritation of the wax, trauma caused by removal, or possibly the ear not being properly dried after syringing.

Discharge

Middle ear discharge in the meatus can cause an external otitis.

Poor hygiene
Poor personal hygiene such as using dirty towels.

Bathing
Swimming, particularly in infected water.

Psychological
Stress and worry may precipitate this condition.

Clinical features
Initially the condition will cause irritation and itching. The meatus will look red and flaky with desquamation of the skin causing debris in the meatus. If it becomes worse there will be pain, the meatus will be red, swollen and raw, probably with a scanty weeping discharge. Deafness will occur because of the debris blocking the meatus and also the swelling.

With a fungal infection there will be a white mass of fungus in the canal. Should the condition become chronic the meatus may become fissured, scarred and stenosed.

Treatment
An aural swab will be sent for culture. The patient must be instructed to keep the ear dry and refrain from scratching. Scratching can cause trauma, allowing secondary bacterial infection and so exacerbates the condition. Aural toilet must be performed regularly to remove the debris.

Aural toilet
This is the term given to the removal of discharge and debris from the ear. It is essential to perform it under direct vision using a headlight and head mirror or possibly an auroscope. Cotton wool wrapped securely round the end of a wool carrier is usually used by trained nursing staff.

It is essential to get the meatus clean before drops or ointment are instilled. These are usually impregnated into a piece of half inch ribbon gauze which is then inserted into the meatus.

Local applications for external otitis are numerous. The choice depends on the causes and whether the condition is allergic or infective. Solutions which are soothing, disinfectant and help clean the meatus are frequently used, for example glycerene and ichthammol, Aluminium Acetate 8%. Steroids such as Hydrocortisone and Betnovate are used topically sometimes combined with antbiotics as in Gentisone HC or Terricortril. Antibiotic drops tend to be avoided. Fungal infections can be difficult to treat because of their ability to form spores. Although they appear to respond quickly, treatment should be continued for several weeks. Nystatin is a commonly used antifungal drug. Associated conditions like dandruff and eczema must be treated and advice given on personal hygiene and about avoiding irritants such as hair sprays. Unfortunately this condition tends to recurr. Eventually the meatus can be scarred and stenosed and a meatoplasty may be necessary.

Practice Questions

Conditions of the outer ear and examination tests

1. What is usually the first symptom of external otitis? Is it
   a itching
   b otalgia
   c deafness
   d otorrhea
2. Fungal infection of the external ear may be treated by using which of the following ear drops?
   a Aluminium Acetate 8%
   b Gentisone HC
   c Nystatin
   d Penicillin
3. A bead in the external auditory meatus will usually be removed by
   a syringing
   b forceps
   c blunt hook
   d instilling warm oil
4. An operation to reconstruct the meatus is called
   a meatoplasty
   b myringotomy
   c myringoplasty
   d tympanoplasty
5. Which of the following refers to a sensori neural deafness?
   a Rinne Test is positive
   b Rinne Test is negative
   c Weber Test is lateralized to deaf ear
   d Air conduction is reduced
6. When performing a caloric test the
   a fluid used is 30° to 37°c
   b ears are irrigated for 30 seconds
   c superior semi-circular canal must be in the horizontal plane
   d lateral semi-circular canal is in the vertical plane
7. What is an aural furuncule?
   What will a patient with this condition complain of?
   How will it be treated?
8. List the possible causes and predisposing factors of external otitis.

9. What are the possible complications of
   — **haematoma** of the pinna
   — **aural foreign body**
   — **wax**
   — **wax solvents**
10. Define otorrhia
    otalgia
    conductive deafness
    sensorineural deafness

Answers

1. **a**
2. **c**
3. **c**
4. **a**
5. **a**
6. **d**
7. An aural furuncule is a staphylococcal infection of a hair follicle in the meatus.

   The patient will complain of irritation, pain, trismus and possibly an enlarged gland and deafness.

   Treatment — local treatment e.g. glycerine and ichthammol, antibiotics, analgesics, aural toilet for removal of discharge. If recurrent, test urine.
8. Causes — predisposing factors of external otitis may include: allergy, trauma, bacterial and fungal infections, skin conditions, wax, middle ear discharge, poor hygiene, water-moisture in the meatus, bathing, psychological factors such as stress.
9. **Haematoma** of the pinna can lead to perichondritis — necrosis of cartilage (cauliflower ear).

   Aural foreign body can cause trauma of the meatus or ear drum, deafness, perforation of ear drum, or could be pushed into the middle of the ear. **Wax** can cause deafness, irritation and sometimes pain. Can predispose to external otitis. **Wax solvents** can cause external otitis.
10. Otorrhoea — ear discharge
    Otalgia — earache
    Conductive deafness — this is deafness which occurs when sound is prevented from reaching the inner ear.
    Sensori-neural deafness — this is deafness caused by conditions affecting the cochlea, auditory nerve, auditory pathways, centres in the brain.

(iii) Conditions of the middle ear
Acute Supperative Otitis Media

Acute supperative otitis media
This is an acute infection of the middle ear cleft and is usually a condition of childhood. It may occur as a complication of an upper respiratory tract infection or of conditions such as influenza and measles. Causal organisms may therefore be bacterial or viral.

The infection usually spreads from the naso pharynx via the Eustachian tube to the middle ear. Less commonly this condition may be caused by a traumatic perforation of the drum or as a result of diving and swimming with a perforation.

Infection in the middle ear will produce an inflammation of the mucosa and a serous exudate which will become pus. The Eustachian tube will also become inflamed and oedematous.

On examination the drum will be seen to be going through stages of becoming pink to red as the vessels become more infected. There will be loss of landmarks as the drum bulges and finally perforates with relief of pain and discharge of pus if treatment does not stop the disease process.

The patient who is usually a child with an upper respiratory tract infection will be obviously ill, pyrexial, have a severe throbbing earache and a degree of deafness.

Treatment
After examination a swob is taken of any discharge and sent for culture and sensitivity. An antibiotic, usually penicillin, is commenced though this may be changed if the swab report shows the organisms to be insensitive. Nasal drops such as ephedrine ½% in normal saline which are decongestents are useful to give vaso constriction and will open up the Eustachian tube.

The nursing care will be that of a pyrexial child, so rest, extra fluids and analgesics are needed. Should the ear be discharging aural toilet can be given. Occasionally a myringotomy may be performed to drain the pus from the middle ear and relieve pain.

If the child is going to be cared for by the parents, at home, the importance of giving the full course of antibiotics must be stressed. Otherwise the condition can become quiescent and cause complications later. Adequately treated the middle ear cleft and the hearing should return to normal. However any predisposing causes of the infection should also be treated or the condition will recurr.

Complications of acute supperative otitis media
Infection may spread to the mastoid air cell giving an acute mastoiditis.

Facial nerve paralysis could occur if the nerve is not covered by bone. Inflammation of the soft tissues over the nerve would cause this.

Only a thin plate of bone separates the middle ear from the temporal lobe of the brain. Infection, usually blood borne can spread upwards causing intracranial complications such as extra dural abscess, meningitis and brain abscess. Similarly infection could go to the inner ear causing a labyrinthitis.

Fortunately with antibiotic therapy these complications are now rare following acute middle ear infection.

Acute mastoiditis

With any acute infection of the middle ear the mucosal lining of the mastoid antrum and air cells will become involved in the inflammatory process. However an acute mastoiditis indicates bony involvement with the partitians beween the cells becoming infected and broken down. This may be because the infection is particularly virulent, the patients resistence is low or the original treatment given was not adequate.

The patient with an acute mastoiditis is ill, pyrexial, has an elevated pulse and increasing deafness. There is otalgia, otorrhea, and oedema can cause sagging of the meatal roof near to the drum. Pain is severe with tenderness over the mastoid process. Swelling behind the ear may push the pinna forward. Abscess formation can occur.

Treatment

Appropriate antibiotic therapy will be given, probably penicillin.

A cortical mastoidectomy may be performed to remove the diseased tissue, provide drainage and prevent further complications. The incision will be post aural and therefore the hair must be shaved above and behind the ear. However with an acute mastoiditis the swelling and tenderness can make this very painful, so it may be left until the patient is anaesthetized.

The mastoid cells and antrum are opened and debris, pus and granulations removed. A drain is put in, the wound closed and the meatus packed. As the middle ear is not touched during the procedure it should return to normal.

A cortical mastoidectomy may be performed electively when it is thought there may be residual infection quiescent after an acute otitis media.

Secretory otitis media

This is a chronic condition of the middle ear often known as ‘glue’ ear. It is a common condition in children of the age group 4–10 when it presents as a conductive deafness.

Causes

This condition is associated with Eustachian tube insufficiency which may be predisposed to by naso-pharyngeal infection, nasal allergy and adenoids.

Otitic baratrauma which occurs in some people when landing in an aircraft may prevent air from going up the Eustachion tube.

The presence of a naso-pharyngeal tumour must be suspected when an adult first presents with this condition.

It is thought that an acute supperative otitis media inadequately treated with antibiotics can cause a middle ear effusion and predispose to secretory otitis media.

When the Eustachian tube is not functioning well the middle ear will be insufficiently aerated. As the air in the middle ear is absorbed a negative pressure is created. This will cause fluid to be drawn into the middle ear from the mucosal glands which will then become thick and more glue like. The negative pressure will also cause the drum to be drawn inward.

On examination the drum is seen to be retracted, looks bluish or yellow and air bubbles or a fluid level may be seen behind. There can be a stuffy uncomfortable feeling in the ear and sometimes otalgia from the retracted drum. The deafness is conductive and can fluctuate causing educational and sometimes behavioural problems.

Treatment

This is directed towards

a Treating the underlying cause.

b Re-aerating the middle ear and preventing permanent changes taking place.

c Improving the hearing and so preventing educational and social problems for the child.

Any nasal allergy is investigated and treated. Nearby infection is treated with antibiotics or surgery, for example tonsillectomy or antrum washouts.

The post-nasal space is examined and any adenoids removed.

Myringotomy is usually done to suck out any fluid in the middle ear. A grommet (Fig. 4) may be put into the myringotomy incision to aerate the middle ear. These are left until they fall out but may be re-introduced if necessary.

The child should receive any remedial help needed to prevent falling behind in their education.

As the child gets older the condition should become self-limiting provided that permanent changes have not taken place in the middle ear cleft.

Fig 4 A grommet

This condition if found in the adult may have remained from childhood. Examination of the naso-pharynx should always be done to exclude a possible tumour.

Chronic supperative otitis media (CSOM)

This is chronic infection of the middle ear which gives rise to deafness, discharge and perforation of the drum. The infection causes the middle ear mucosa to become thickened with granulation and some times aural polyp formation. An aural polyp is oedematous pedunculated mucosa which extends through the perforated drum and can be seen in the external meatus.

Chronic supperative otitis media is usually divided into two types, each known by several names.

Simple-mucosal-tube tympanic CSOM

Dangerous-bony-attico-antral CSOM

Simple CSOM does not cause serious complications and is usually associated with naso-pharyngeal infection. The discharge is muco-purulent and intermittent, dry for a period and then recurring when the ear gets wet or the patient has a cold. There is a central perforation. The deafness varies according to the degree of damage which has been done to the ossicles by the disease. Invariably the incus is affected first.

Treatment

The aim of this is to cure the infection and improve the hearing. Any nearby sepsis is treated. Local treatment in the form of aural toilet and the instillation of topical drops or powders are given to get the ear dry. Micro toilet, that is, cleaning the ear under an operating microscope, is often undertaken in the out patients department or theatre.

Aural polypi can be removed, usually under a general anaesthetic.

When the ear is dry and the Eustachion tube functioning reconstructive surgery can be undertaken.

Dangerous CSOM is associated with complications and can be life threatening. The discharge tends to be scanty and foul smelling, the perforation is marginal and the deafness severe. Nearby bone can become eroded by infection and cholesteatoma allowing the infection to spread. A fistula into the lateral semi-circular canal could cause a labyrinthitis and destruction of part of the bony facial canal with a facial paralysis. Intracranial complications such as extra dural abscess, lateral sinus thrombosis, meningitis and brain abscess could occur.

Cholesteatoma is skin in the middle ear which has migrated from the meatus through a perforation, or has been formed from a retraction pocket when the upper part of the drum has been sucked inwards due to negative pressure in the middle ear.

Cholesteatoma is a white cheesy substance with a characteristic smell which has the ability to erode bone thus damaging the ossicles and opening up pathways for infection to spread.

Treatment

Treatment of the dangerous type of CSOM is usually surgical and aims to make the ear safe.

Conservative treatment such as micro toilet can be given to get the ear dry and so improve the chances or surgery.

When a patient presents with an acute exacerbation of this condition with pain or any indication of complications surgery usually has to be undertaken at once.

Surgery for chronic middle ear infection

Mastoidectomy

In this operation the diseased and infected tissue and bone is removed leaving a cavity. Incision is either post aural or endaural. The mastoid antrum is opened, the mastoid and middle ear are made into a cavity leaving the facial nerve covered by bone.

In the traditional radical mastoidectomy the drum and all of the ossicles except the stapes are removed. However, with a modified radical mastoidectomy there is preservation of as much of the undiseased middle ear contents as is possible.

The cavity will be packed with ½ inch ribbon gauze impregnated with a substance such as BIPP (bismuth iodiform paraffin paste) A BIPP pack has the advantage that it can be left in for some time without becoming foul. Some surgeons may put siliastic sheet in before the BIPP. The wound is sutured and a dressing, pad and firm bandage applied.

The pack is changed by the medical staff. Gradually the cavity will epithelize.

Although the mastoidectomy will give the patient a safe ear they will nevertheless have a hearing loss — also a cavity which will need periodic cleaning and which may discharge intermittently.

Tympanoplasty

The operation of tympanoplasty is designed to reconstruct the middle ear and so improve hearing. It must however be carried out on a safe ear preferably a dry one.

Tympanoplasty is the repair of the drum perforation and the reconstruction of the defects in the ossicular chain. The exact form of the operation will depend on the individual ear, the extent of the disease process and the personal techniques preferred by the surgeon.

Tympanoplasties are sometimes graded, the simplest form, or grade 1, being a myringoplasty which is repair of the drum perforation. Fascia from the temporalis muscle which is readily accessible over the ear is used for the graft to repair the drum. A bed is first prepared for the fascia by depithelization of the drum remains, so ensuring skin cannot grow into the middle ear. The graft is laid either over or under the perforation, the meatus packed and the incision sutured.

Other types of tympanoplasty will include ossicular reconstruction as well as drum repair. This may take the form of, for example, an interposition of incus using a strut of cartilage or bone to support the graft/or placing the graft to get acoustic separation of the oval and round windows. Some surgeons prefer the operation to be done in two stages. First ensuring the ear is disease free and then doing the final reconstruction some months later.

Otosclerosis

This is a condition of the middle ear where there is abnormal growth of new spongy bone laid down mainly round the foot-plate of the stapes causing it to become fixed.

The cause is unknown. It occurs in young adults, is more common in white than coloured races, fair rather than dark individuals and there is often a family history. More female than males appear to present with the condition probably because it is usually made worse by pregnancy. Fixation of the stapes will cause deafness which is progressive and usually bi-lateral. The patient may be aware that they can hear better in noisy surroundings, a condition called **paracusis.** They may also complain of tinnitus.

On examination the tympanic membrane will look normal or have a pinkish tinge. Audiometry will show a conductive deafness sometimes with a bone conduction dip at 200 Hz. Otosclerotic changes may also occur in the cochlea giving a mixed deafness.

Treatment

After careful explanation of the nature of the condition and the fact that it is no way life threatening, the patient is told that they may be fitted with a hearing aid and possibly have the help of lip reading lessons or have surgery.

Stapedectomy is the operation offered for this condition. However, as this is purely elective surgery it is always pointed out that there is a small risk of complete deafness due to the operation. Surgery is always performed on the worst ear though patients may later wish for the second ear to be operated on.

Pre-operatively the patient must be free of any infection to minimise the risk of post-operative labyrinthitis.

Stapedectomy may be done under a local or general anaesthetic using the operating microscope and a meatal speculum. The meatus may be enlarged with an endaural incision.

An incision is made in the deep posterior meatal wall and the drum reflected. After exposure of the ossicles the diagnosis can be confirmed by touching the fixed stapes. The incudo stapedius joint is disarticulated and the head and crura of the stapes removed. A hole is made in the footplate and the prosthesis is fitted. Prostheses come in various types usually of teflon or stainless steel.

They basically have a strut which fits into the hole in the stapes footplate and a hook which is attached to the incus. There are different sizes to accommodate individual middle ears. When the prosthesis is in place the drum is replaced and a meatal pack left in. Any incision is sutured and a piece of cotton wool left covering the pack. A pad and bandage is not usually necessary.

Care of patients having Middle Ear surgery

Pre-operative

The specific preoperative care of a patient admitted for middle ear surgery will be an ENT examination and hearing tests including audiometry. Unless the operation is urgent mastoid surgery it is desirable the patient should be free of active upper respiratory tract infection to lesson the risk of post operative complications.

An appropriate ear shave is done depending upon the operation. Usually only a minimal amount of hair is removed, the remainder is taped out of the way in theatre. As the patient has a hearing loss it is important to check that they have understood any explanations given.

Post-operative

All the usual care is taken to recover the patient safely from the anaesthetic. The patient should be watched in the immediate post-operative period for any indication of hypotension. It is often the practice when doing middle ear surgery using the operating microscope for the anaesthetist to lower the blood pressure with the aid of drugs. This is to give a virtually bloodless field to facilitate the delicate surgery involved. Therefore post-operatively the blood pressure may have not returned to normal.

After middle ear surgery it is important to ensure that the facial nerve is intact by checking there are equal and full movements of the face. This establishes there has been no surgical trauma to the nerve. Any paralysis occuring later will probably be due to oedema or pressure from a pack. Facial paralysis may sometimes be seen with a stapedectomy done under a local anaesthetic, due to the drugs, but recovery takes place quickly.

Patients having middle ear surgery are nursed with the operated ear uppermost, usually with only one pillow at first. Analgesics are given for any pain though patients tend to complain little about this. However they are often nauseated and giddy when the inner ear has been disturbed. After stapedectomy giddiness may go on for several days, labyrinthine suppressents such as stemetil are given as required.

Oral fluid may be commenced as soon as the patient feels able. Normal diet given the following day. Patients with their head on one side will require some help at mealtimes and their drinks are most easily taken from a feeding cup and straw.

The usual check is made that the patient is passing urine, particularly as they may have difficulty while lying down.

The day following mastoid surgery or tympanoplasty the patient can usually mobilise gradually, as they feel able. Assistance will be given with hygiene at first but patients are usually self-caring very quickly. After stapedectomy patients generally stay in bed for two to three days being sat up one pillow at a time. They will need the care necessary for a patient at bedrest who has to keep their head fairly still.

Patients who have had reconstructive middle ear surgery are advised to avoid coughing sneezing or blowing the nose for a while. Also sudden movements of the head when they do get up.

After mastoid surgery or tympanoplasty the wound should be watched for any oozing. The dressing can be taken down first day and may be redressed with a light dessing, or the sutures just sprayed with a dressing spray. Any drain such as in a cortical mastoidectomy would be removed when the drainage is minimal — about 2–3 days. Sutures in any operation would be ready for removal from 5 days. Meatal wool is changed as necessary but packs are usually changed or removed by medical staff.

It is important for nursing staff to observe for any indication of infection, swelling, pyrexia, increased pain or giddiness. Labyrinthitis after stapedectomy could mean a totally deaf ear.

Patients having surgery to improve hearing may find the hearing improves initially and then may go off. They should be reassured. Fluctuation can occur and the full effect of the operation may not be felt for some time.

Usually discharge from hospital is about the seventh day with follow up as outpatients. The patients are advised on the importance of keeping their ear dry and avoiding situations where they may feel giddy.

Practice Questions

The middle ear

1. A six-year-old child is admitted with secretory otitis media. Admission will have been advised because of:
   a Otalgia
   b Otorrhea
   c Conductive deafness
   d Sensory neural deafness
2. Which of the following may have predisposed to this condition?
   a Nasal allergy
   b External otitis
   c Swimming
   d Perforated ear drum
3. On examination the tympanic membrane will most likely be:
   a Bulging
   b Injected
   c Perforated
   d Retracted
4. A myringotomy is performed and the fluid from the ear will most probably be:
   a Pus
   b Serous
   c Blood stained
   d Thick mucous
5. A grommet is inserted. The function of which is to
   a Drain middle ear fluid
   b Aerate the middle ear

c Allow sound to pass through
d Support the tympanic membrane

6. The grommet will probably stay in until
a It falls out
b It is removed
c There is no more discharge
d Drum returns to normal
7. A 4-year-old child is seen in the out-patient department with a severe ear ache, pyrexia and a heavy cold. The child will most likely be found to have a
a Secretory otitis media
b Acute supperative otitis media
c CSOM
d Aural furuncle
8. On examination the tympanic membrane is seen to
a Be retracted
b Be pearly grey
c Show of air bubbles behind
d Be red and injected
9. Treatment ordered is likely to be
a Ampicillin and decongestent nasal drops
b Ampicillin and antibiotic ear drops
c Myringotomy and insertion of grommet
d Myringotomy and antbiotic ear drops
10. The most common complication which could follow this condition would be
a Acute mastoiditis
b Labyrinthitis
c Facial paralysis
d Extra dural abscess
11. What advice would you give to the mother regarding the care of the child?
12. Explain briefly:
a Cholesteatoma
b Aural polyp
c Otosclerosis
d Tympanoplasty
e Myringoplasty
f Micro toilet
g CSOM
h Modified radical mastoidectomy
13. What are the complications which could occur with
a Cholesteatoma
b Stapedectomy

c CSOM — bony type
d Retracted drum

14. What specific pre-operative preparation will a patient need who is to have middle ear surgery.
15. Describe the specific post-operative care of a patient after tympanoplasty.
16. What advice can be given to a patient going home after stapedectomy?

Answers

1. **c**
2. **a**
3. **d**
4. **d**
5. **b**
6. **a**
7. **b**
8. **d**
9. **a**
10. **a**
11. Advise the mother to:
    a (Preferably) keep the child in bed
    b Give plenty of fluids
    c Tepid sponge if child is very hot
    d The full course of the anti-biotics must be given
    e Instil nasal drops as instructed
    f Analgesia suitable of the childs age e.g. junior aspirin
    g Who to contact if the symptoms get worse, subside then recurr, or do not subside fairly quickly, or any problem such as swelling behind the ear occurs.
12. Cholesteatoma is skin in the middle ear
    — appears as a white cheesy substance
    — skin has migrated through a perforation to form a retraction pocket.
    Aural polypi is oedematous pedunculated mucosa arising in the middle ear, protruding through a perforation in the drum.
    Otosclerosis — condition where there is formation of new spongy bone mainly around the footplate of the stapes.
    Tympanoplasty — operation for reconstruction of the middle ear to improve hearing, usually reconstruction of the drum and the ossicular chain.
    Myringoplasty — reconstruction of the tympanic membrane usually with temporal fascia.

Micro-toilet — is examination of the ear and aural toilet using the operating microscope.
CSOM — chronic middle ear infection with symptoms of deafness, discharge and perforation of the drum. Can be divided into two types — simple or mucosal and dangerous or bony.
Modified Radical Mastoidectomy — the middle ear and mastoid are made into a cavity, all the diseased infected tissue being removed.

13. Cholesteatoma is able to erode bone and so can cause destruction in the middle ear, may erode the facial canal through to the inner ear and the brain, allowing infection to spread.
Stapedectomy can be complicated by labyrinthitis, complete deafness.
CSOM — could cause facial palsy, labyrinthitis, intra-cranial complications.
Retracted drum can lead to formation of a retraction pocket and skin migrating into the middle ear causing cholesteatoma.
14. ENT examination
— audiometry
— minimal shave as is appropriate
— should be free from active upper respiratory tract infection if possible
— give appropriate explanation of post-operative care
— ensure the patient has heard and therefore understood.
15. The post-operative care of a patient after tympanoplasty may include:
— safe recovery from anaesthetic
— observe for any hypotension
— check the facial nerve is intact
— give analgesic as required
— labyrinthine suppresents for nausea and giddiness
— nurse with operated ear uppermost
— oral fluids as desired
— normal diet first day
— check patient is passing urine
— check dressing for any oozing
— 1st day remove dressing and bandage
— replace with light dressing and/or spray
— change meatal wool daily as necessary
— sutures removed from 5th day
— meatal pack removed by medical staff
— assist with hygiene at first
— gradually mobilise from 1st day
— avoiding sudden head movements

— advise patient to avoid coughing, sneezing, blowing nose
— watch for any indication of infection e.g. pyrexia, increased pain, dizziness and swelling
— warn patient their hearing may fluctuate.

16. Advise patient to:
— take things easy until seen again
— avoid coming in contact with infection
— continue to avoid coughing, sneezing, blowing the nose if possible
— avoid sudden head movements, it may cause giddiness
— avoid situations where giddiness could be dangerous — like going up a ladder
— warn them hearing may fluctuate
— advise who to contact if they are worried or if anything appears to be wrong e.g. sudden deafness
— they will be seen as out-patients for follow-up.

(iv) Conditions of the inner ear

Conditions of the inner ear may present with symptoms of deafness, vertigo and tinnitus.

Deafness — is sensori-neural.

Vertigo — the hallucination of movement may at times be accompanied by nausea and vomiting.

Tinnitus — the sensation of noise in the ears or head.

The inner ear may be affected by such problems as congenital abnormalities, trauma, infection, drugs and the ageing process.

Congenital abnormalities

A baby may be born with a damaged inner ear and sensori-neural deafness. The cause may be hereditory, associated with other congenital abnormalities, or unknown. Again the mother could have been exposed during pregnancy to a viral infection like rubella, toxins from drugs or there may be Rhesus incompatability. Prematurity, birth injuries, anoxia, or even being long term in an incubator can cause inner ear damage in the new born.

Trauma

This may be physical trauma which may occur if the inner ear is involved in a head injury or blast injury which could rupture the cochlea.

Noise

Prolonged exposure to noise above 90dB can cause acoustic trauma. This will commonly occur in industry, or being in the vicinity of large machines such as aircraft. In recent years the problem has become recognised and legislation has been introduced to protect personel either

by shielding the machinery if possible and providing ear protectors. Unfortunately the latter are not always made full use of. Compensation can be claimed for deafness caused in this way.
The modern practice of amplifying pop music to the volume which is common in discotheque may well be causing cochlea damage in young people who are regularly exposing themselves to this noise.

Drugs
Certain drugs are known to be ototoxic these include streptomycin, neomycin, gentomycin, chlorhexidine, aspirin, quinine, some diurectics and cytotoxic drugs. Patients on these drugs should be monitered and nurses should always be aware of this side effect. Any evidence of dizziness, tinnitus or indication of deafness should be reported.

Presbycusis
Presbycusis is sensori neural deafness which occurs with the normal ageing process. The higher frequencies being affected first. It is probably caused by diminished blood supply to the inner ear.

Infection
Inner ear deafness can be caused by exposure to infections such as measles, mumps, meningitis, labyrinthitis and other viral diseases.

Acoustic Neuroma
This is a neuroma of the viii cranial nerve usually arising in the internal auditory meatus. Although this is a benign tumour it is potentially life threatening because of its position at the cerebral pontine angle. As it enlarges it will involve the vii and v cranial nerves, cerebellum, and eventually the brain stem.

The patient will present usually with inner symptoms, deafness, tinnitus and vertigo. Later there would be facial weakness loss of sensation over one side of the face, absence of the corneal reflex and pain. This could progress to ataxia, signs of raised intra cranial pressure and eventually brain stem involvement.

Otological, vestibular and neurological investigations would be carried out. Diagnosis will generally be confirmed by scanning and X-ray, showing an enlarged internal auditory meatus.

Treatment is by surgical removal. A small neuroma confined to the internal auditory meatus may be accessible by a middle ear approach. Usually however a craniotomy is necessary and therefore the patient is referred to the neuro-surgical unit. Operation will usually leave the patient with a facial paralysis. Sometimes a middle ear and craniotomy combined approach may be made. The patient will generally be nursed in the neuro surgery unit.

Ménières disease

Ménières disease is a condition of the inner ear where the patient experiences a triad of symptoms: tinnitus, deafness and vertigo.

There are sudden episodic attacks of giddiness accompanied usually by nausea and vomiting. The attack varies in severity, duration and frequency.

The deafness is sensori-neural often with distortion of sound. Before and during an attack of vertigo the deafness tends to get worse but will usually improve afterwards. However there is a slow but progressive deterioration.

Tinnitus is often the first symptom to appear and probably the most distressing for many patients. It also tends to get worse with an attack.

The onset of Ménières is usually at middle age and may be unilateral or bilateral. Although it is known there is an excess of fluid in the membranous labyrinth in this condition why it occurs is not understood.

Ménières disease is extremely distressing and worrying for the patient as they often equate the symptoms with a possible brain tumour.

Investigation

Audiometry will show a sensori neural deafness. Caloric tests will demonstrate a canal paresis on the affected side. Neurological investigations should be carried out to eliminate other possible causes of the symptoms such as Acoustic Neuroma.

Treatment

After the diagnosis is confirmed the patient will be reassured they do not have a brain tumour and an explanation of Ménières disease is given to them.

Drug therapy is usually the first mode of treatment. Labyrinthine suppressents such as Stemetil (prochlorperazine) can be used during an attack. Prophylactically the drug most commonly used is Serc (betahistine hydrochloride). Sedatives such as phenobarbitone and vasodilators may also be prescribed.

Surgery may have to be considered if drugs fail to help the patient sufficiently. Various operations have been devised for decompressing the labyrinth but are not widely used. Selective destruction of the labyrinth where there is some useful residual hearing may be carried out.

In unilateral cases where there is little useful hearing left and the patients symptoms are not being controlled adequately by drugs labyrinthectomy can be carried out.

Labyrinthectomy

A cortical mastoidectomy is performed and the membraneous labyrinth destroyed through a hole drilled in the lateral semi-circular canal.

Post-operatively the care is the same as for patients having any middle ear surgery. However, the patients are giddy for some time so will need adequate drugs to control this. They will be nursed in bed at first then very gradually mobilized, care being taken for their safety. Special exercises are given by the physiotherapists to help regain balance.

The opposite labyrinth will, after a while, compensate. However on discharge the patient should be advised to be careful when in the dark or in any potentially dangerous situation.

Labyrinthitis

Labyrinthitis is infection of the inner ear. It can occur as a complication to acute middle ear infection but is more likely to follow CSOM.

Infection may gain access to the inner ear in several ways

a Through a fistula in the lateral semi-circular canal eroded by cholesteatoma. Here the patients have a positive fistula sign. This means they become giddy when the external auditory meatus is compressed due to the change in pressure.

b Directly via the oval or round windows. A possible complication of acute suppurative otitis media.

c Blood borne usually again from acute middle ear infection.

d Trauma as a result of injury involving the inner ear.

e Post-operatively after surgical intervention, for example stapedectomy.

f Secondary to meningeal infection through the internal auditory meatus.

At first the patient will have the signs and symptoms of the pre-existing condition plus those of labyrinthine irritation which are vertigo, nausea, vomiting, nystagmus.

As the condition progresses the symptoms will vary accordingly.

During the inflammatory stage the patient will experience vertigo which may be accompanied by nausea and vomiting. Nystagmus may also be present.

Further irritation can produce sudden attacks of vertigo and vomiting. The patient will be curled up on the unaffected side with eyes closed or turned towards the affected ear. Should they stand up they would fall to the opposite side. They are deaf but still have some hearing.

With pus formation in the labyrinth the symptoms will get worse and the patient more toxic. The direction of the nystagmus will change as the labyrinth becomes paralysed and the ear will become completely deaf.

Finally the labyrinth will die. There will be complete neuro-sensory deafness which will never recover or improve. However the loss of vestibular function will be compensated for later.

Adequate treatment will hopefully prevent this situation occurring. Antibiotic therapy will be given. When the cause is a CSOM exploration of the middle ear and removal of cholesteatoma will be undertaken.

Nursing care

The patient will be in bed and lying still to lessen the vertigo. Therefore, they will need all the nursing care of a patient confined to bed and all the usual measures must be taken to prevent the complications of bed rest (See *Principles of Nursing* in this series).

Antibiotics and labyrinthine suppressents are given as prescribed. A drug such as Stemetil will help lessen the vertigo and also act as an anti-emetic.

Fluid intake is monitored and if the patient is vomiting, small frequent drinks are probably more easily retained. Intravenous fluid could be necessary if they appear to be getting dehydrated.

Cot sides are generally put up while the patient is giddy.

When the vertigo has lessened the patient can be mobilized gradually, with care for their safety.

Practice Questions

1. List possible causes of congenital deafness.
2. List possible causes of acquired sensori-neural deafness.
3. What are:
   tinnitus
   vertigo
   nystagmus
   positive fistula sign
4. What are the triad of symptoms of Ménières disease. Is it?
   a deafness, tinnitus, vomiting
   b tinnitus, vertigo, nystagmus
   c deafness, tinnitus, vertigo
   d deafness, nystagmus, vomiting
5. Which of the following are ototoxic drugs
   i gentamycin
   ii aspirin
   iii neomycin
   iv erythromycin
   Is it
   a i ii iii
   b ii iii iv
   c i iii iv
   d all of them?

6. What is the most likely cause of labyrinthitis? Is it:
   a acute suppurative otitis media
   b acute mastoiditis
   c CSOM — bony type
   d CSOM — mucosal type?
7. Méniѐres disease is a condition where there is:
   a increased endolymph
   b decreased endolymph
   c increased perilymph
   d decreased perilymph
8. Betahistine Hydrocholride (Serc) is a drug often used in the treatment of:
   a acoustic neuroma
   b presbyacusis
   c labyrinthitis
   d Méniѐres disease
9. An acoustic neuroma can be life threatening because:
   a of its position at the cerebello-pontine angle
   b it is a malignant tumour
   c it can quickly cause raised intra-cranial pressure
   d it can erode through the internal auditory meatus
10. Using a problem solving approach plan the care of a patient with labyrinthitis, giving reasons for this care.

Answers

1. Possible causes of congenital deafness:
   hereditary
   maternal infection e.g. rubella
   maternal drug toxins
   birth injury anoxia
   Rhesus incompatability
   unknown causes
2. Causes of acquired sensori-neural deafness include
   infections e.g. measles
   noise trauma
   ototoxic drugs
   presyacusis
   Méniѐres disease
   acoustic neuroma
   condition affecting auditory pathway and centres in the brain
3. Tinnitus — the sensation of noise in the ears or head.
   Vertigo — hallucination of movement.
   Nystagmus — involuntary rapid eye movements.

Positive Fistula Sign — compressing the meatus will induce vertigo, indicating a fistula from the middle ear to the labyrinth.

4. **c**
5. **a**
6. **c**
7. **a**
8. **d**
9. **a**

10. CARE PLAN FOR PATIENT WITH LABYRINTHITIS

PROBLEMS	NURSING CARE	REASON
Vertigo	Nurse patient in a position where giddiness is least disturbing Labyrinthine suppressents as ordered, e.g. Stemetil	Control giddiness
Nausea Vomiting	Give antiemetics — e.g. Stemetil Small frequent drinks Food as able or desired Intravenous infusion if oral fluids not adequate	Maintain hydration and nutrition
May have dry mouth	Assist with oral hygiene	Prevent oral infection Maintain patient's comfort
Infection	Record temperature and pulse 4 hourly antibiotics as prescribed	Monitor condition Control infection
Limited mobility due to giddiness	Assist with hygiene Care of pressure areas Encourage leg movement and deep breathing	Maintain hygiene and comfort Prevent the complications of bed rest
Deafness	Stand in a position where the patient can see you Ensure that the patient has understood	Prevent breakdown of communication and patient's isolation
Risk of Falling	Use of cot side Everything positioned within reach Gradual mobilization with adequate help	Ensure patient's safety

3 DEAFNESS

Deafness may be conductive, sensori-neural, or if both occur together will be known as a mixed deafness.

Conductive deafness will involve the external or middle ear while sensori-neural may be related to the cochlea, auditory nerve, auditory pathway or centres in the brain.

Causes

Deafness may be congenital or acquired and the causes are numerous.

Causes of conductive deafness include:

wax
external otitis
foreign bodies in the meatus
perforation of the ear drum
acute suppurative otitis media
secretory otitis media
CSOM
otosclerosis
dislocation of ossicular chain
tumours of the external and middle ear
congenital abnormalities of the external and middle ear.

Causes of sensori-neural deafness include:

— congential
— hereditary
maternal infection e.g. Rubella
maternal drug toxins
birth trauma and anoxia
Rhesus incompatability
unknown

Infections e.g. measles, mumps, meningitis, labyrinthitis
Injuries e.g. head injuries, blast
Noise e.g. industrial
Ototoxic Drugs
Presbyausis
Ménière's Disease
Acoustic neuromas
Central nervous system conditions
Otosclerotic change in the cochlea

Effects of a hearing loss

A hearing loss can be a terrible handicap yet on the whole the deaf do not get the sympathy, understanding and help which is given to the blind or other physically disabled people. Society has always had a tendency to treat deaf people as difficult, tiresome and stupid. They in turn will feel isolated, frustrated, irritable and lonely. Hearing people tend not really to understand the full implications of a hearing loss, especially of the sensori neural type.

With a conductive deafness sounds are heard quietly and there is quite often the ability to hear better in noisy surroundings. Speech remains normal because the individual can hear and monitor their own voice.

Children with a conductive deafness such as that caused by secretory otitis will have acquired normal speech but could have educational problems because of being unable to hear the teachers. They may present behavioural problems and find peer contact difficult because of the attitude of other children. Conditions causing conductive deafness can have appropriate medical or surgical treatment. Awareness by the parents and teachers can mean, for instance, the child sitting in the right place in class and receiving any remedial help necessary.

A hearing aid may in some cases be provided. With help, a child with a conductive deafness should be able to cope and reach its full educational potential.

An adult will have similar problems. The inability to hear can cause breakdown in communication and embarrassment thus affecting employment, social and family life. Listening needs hard work and concentration and is tiring, so there is a tendency to become uncommunicative and isolated. With appropriate treatment and possible middle ear reconstruction the condition usually can be improved. Otherwise a hearing aid can be of value and possible lip-reading classes.

With a sensori neural deafness adults can have all these problems and more. High frequency sounds are lost first and as these are the consonants speech is heard not only quietly but is also distorted. They cannot hear their own voice so their speech will lose intonation and become flat. Tinnitus is often an additional problem. Recruitment may be experienced which means loud sounds will be heard normally or louder than normal. Shouting can therefore be painfully loud to them. Nurses must remember that many of their elderly patients have some degree of sensori neural hearing loss. Nothing as yet can be done to treat this type of deafness. A hearing aid, help with lip reading and perhaps speech therapy can be given.

Nurses will come in contact with deaf people wherever they work. Therefore they should have an understanding of the effect of the hearing loss, should know how to talk to the person and know the basic care of the hearing aid.

When talking to deaf people in order to help lip reading:

Stand in front of the person with the light on your face.

Attract their attention so that they are listening.

Speak slightly more slowly and distinctively.

Don't cover your mouth.

Don't shout.

If they have not heard try using different words, some lip patterns are easier than others.

The use of natural gestures will often reinforce words.

Remember lip reading is difficult — so be patient.

Hearing aids

The basic function of a hearing aid is to amplify sound and so it is made up of a microphone, amplifier and loudspeaker.

Aids may be body worn or at ear level. A body worn aid is more powerful but can be conspicious and pick up clothes rub. The ear level aid is smaller, but may feel heavy when worn for some time. All aids have the disadvantage that they pick up and amplify ambient noise.

Ear moulds are designed to suit the individual and should fit well in the meatus. The mould can alter the frequency response of the aid by its diameter and length in the meatus. An aid will whistle with acoustic feed back if the mould is not properly in place. Patients with skin conditions may need to be provided with anti-irritant moulds.

Aids are powered by batteries and therefore should always be turned off when not in use. A nurse should understand the control, be able to change the battery and generally look after the aid if patients are not able to do this themselves.

A hearing aid is a very important possession of a patient so should be handled carefully and kept safe for the patient when it is not in their personal care.

There are now a number of modifications to hearing aids and so a greater range available to suit individual people.

Assessment of children

A new born baby will respond to sound with a 'mora start'. At risk babies should be tested at birth.

New born babies can now be tested using a Lincoln Bennett Cradle but at present these are not widely used.

At two months the baby will turn the eyes to sound, at six months the head. This fact is used for the first routine screening or distraction test. This test is carried out by the Health Visitor when the child is able to sit freely on the mother's lap. An observer attracts the baby's attention while the tester makes appropriate noises quietly each side of the baby but out of the line of vision. The baby should turn to the sound. Should the child fail the test on two occasions referral will be made to an otologist.

Children between the age of 2-4 can be tested in a play situation. Sounds are presented at known frequencies and intensities and the child has to make an appropriate response. At five they can be tested by pure tones audiometry. Children are screened twice at school by audiometry sweep tests, one at about five on entry and again when going into junior school at about seven. Hopefully any child with a hearing loss will be picked up by the age of eight.

Children who have been referred are assessed with more extensive tests such as impedence audiometry.

A normal hearing baby begins to associate sounds with objects, voice with faces and finds that when it vocalises people respond. The child imitates the sounds it hears and these begin to have meaning so speech and language as a means of communication is established. Spoken words are linked and sentences made.

It appears to be necessary for a child to be in a hearing environment before language can be learnt because listening seems to be an acquired skill. The first 2-3 years of life seem to be the most important time for the development of speech and understanding language. Therefore it is essential for a child with a congenital loss to be picked up as early as possible. Then a hearing aid can be fitted to get as much sound as possible to the residual hearing so that this period of auditory discrimination development can be utilised.

Once the child is diagnosed and fitted with an aid the mother will be the person who will give the pre school child the most help. She will be guided and advised by a peripatetic teacher of the deaf who will teach her how to help the child with lip reading and acquiring language. Caring for the child's aid and ensuring they wear them is also part of the parents responsibility.

There is now an increasing use of radio hearing aids or phonic ears. These run on radio frequencies and the mother wears a microphone — her speech being picked up by the child's aid.

There must be continual monitoring of the child's progress by the teacher and the otologist.

Children with a hearing loss usually go to school before the statutory age. Finding the right placement for the individual child's education is the most important decision.

Education

Children with a hearing loss of 70-80 dB will for the most part be educated in a school for the deaf. These schools are built to give the best acoustic advantage and are fitted with every means of amplification. They are staffed by teachers of the deaf and the statutory size of the class is less than ten. The teachers must continue the children's auditory training and language development as well as give formal education. Many schools in this country now use 'signed English' as an additional form of communication.

Transport to and from school is provided by the Local Authorities. However, children living in rural areas may have to be weekly boarders.

A 'partial hearing child' is one who has some naturally acquired speech and will include children who have a hearing loss after having learned some language.

These children may be educated at Partial Hearing Schools or Units, or at ordinary schools. The school and units are also purpose built and staffed by teachers of the deaf. Units being attached to ordinary schools give the children the advantage of being able to mix with hearing children. This form of education caters for children with a wide range of hearing and varying academic abilities, the one often compensating for the other.

Some children whose hearing loss is not too great and who are intellectually able can be educated at ordinary schools. These children will be visited by a peripatetic teacher who will monitor their progress. The present trend is wherever possible, to educate handicapped children in ordinary schools, with support. Therefore, in future more children may have the opportunity to be educated with their hearing peers.

Although the facilities for educating hearing impaired children follow a similar pattern throughout the country Local Authorities will make provisions to meet individual local needs. There should, however, always be means of free movement between the places of education to provide what is best for an individual child.

Many children may spend their entire school life at a school for the deaf. Higher education is provided at present in only a very few centres and places are competed for by examination. Very few are able to reach university. The majority of children born with a severe hearing loss are not usually able to reach their full educational potential.

On leaving school the child who has been entirely educated within the close confines of a special school may have difficulty in integrating and finding employment. Many areas of employment are closed to them unfairly as many deaf people have the advantage of being able to concentrate and not be distracted.

Integration into the hearing world can be difficult, especially if their speech is poor and much depends on if they are accepted or shunned by society. Some may feel rejected and return to the organisations and societies for the deaf where they will communicate by signing. The majority will seek acceptance into the hearing world, acknowledge their own limitations and live a full life within the restriction their hearing loss places upon them.

There are many organisations providing help for people with a hearing loss and their families, including the National Deaf Children Society and the Royal National Institute for the Deaf.

Practice Questions

1. Which of the following is a cause of conductive deafness. Is it?
   a Meniérès disease
   b Acoustic trauma
   c Presbyacusis
   d Otosclerosis
2. Which of these indicates a conductive deafness?
   a Weber test lateralised to the deaf ear
   b Rinne test is positive
   c Bone conduction is reduced
   d Sound is distorted
3. Which of the following is related to a sensori neural hearing loss?
   a Low frequencies are usually lost first
   b Speech is not affected
   c Tinnitus often occurs
   d Can be treated surgically
4. When you talk to a deaf person you should?
   a Shout loudly
   b Speak very slowly
   c Keep repeating the same words
   d Use natural gestures
5. All hearing aids have the disadvantage of:
   a Picking up and amplifying ambient sounds
   b Are very conspicious
   c Pick up clothes rub
   d Whistle for no reason
6. List possible causes of conductive deafness.
7. What is?
   a Paracusis
   b Presbyacusis
   c Recruitment
   d A partial hearing child
8. What are the routine tests for screening children's hearing?

9. What is?
   a Lincoln Bennett Cradle
   b A phonic ear
   c An audiogram
10. What are the possible effects of a hearing loss on an adult?
11. What are the effects of congenital deafness on a child?
12. What facilities are available to aid the development and education of a child with a congenital deafness?

Answers

1. **d**
2. **a**
3. **c**
4. **d**
5. **a**
6. Wax
   Inflammation of the meatus, e.g. external otitis
   Foreign bodies
   Perforated ear drum
   Otitis media — acute, suppurative; secretory — C.S.O.M.
   Otosclerosis
   Dislocation of ossicular chain
   Tumours of external and middle ear
   Congenital abnormalities of external or middle ear
7. Paracusis — the ability to hear better in noisy surroundings
   Presbyacusis — deafness which is part of the ageing process
   Recruitment — experiencing loud sounds as loud if not louder than normal
   Partial hearing child — a child with a hearing loss but with some naturally acquired speech.
8. Distraction tests at 7-10 months
   Audiometry sweep tests at school — on school entry and when going into junior school, that is, about 5-7 years.
9. Lincoln Bennett Cradle — special cradle which can be used to test the hearing of the new born.
   Phonic ears — hearing aids which run on radio frequencies
   Audiograms — a chart which is plotted to show the result of a hearing test done by audiometry.
10. Effects of a hearing loss in an adult can be as follows:
    breakdown of communication, embarrassment, isolation, irritation, frustration. Listening is hard work. Affects social, family life and employment.
    If hearing loss is sensori-neural additional problems may be tinnitus,

recruitment, distortion of sound, inability to monitor own voice — loses intonation.

11. A child with a congenital hearing loss:
    does not develop speech and language naturally
    lacks the ability to communicate adequately
    may have behavioural problems
    will be isolated and lonely
    is educationally backwards
    has difficulty with integrating with hearing peers
    may be shunned for being different
    not able to reach their full potential
12. Early assessment diagnosis.
    Testing of 'at risk' neonates (new born).
    Hearing aid fitted.
    Family taught how to help with auditory training, encourage lip reading and linguistic development.
    Family helped and supported by peripatetic teacher of the deaf.
    Continual monitoring of child by otologists and educationalists.
    Careful choice of educational placement.
    Will start school early.

Education facilities available:
- School for the deaf.
- School or unit for partial hearing child.
- Ordinary school with peripatetic help.
- Free movement between places of education
- schools and units staffed by teachers of the deaf
- built with every acoustic advantage and means of amplification.
- Small classes.
- Higher education available by competitive examination.
- Local authorities cater for local needs.
- Voluntary organisations e.g. National Deaf Children's Society.

4 THE NOSE AND PARANASAL SINUSES

The objectives of this section are to:

1. Outline the structure and function of the nose and sinuses.
2. Describe the more common conditions of the nose and sinuses.
3. Explain the relevant care of Patients suffering from these conditions.

Nose

The nose is the first part of the respiratory tract. It has two parts, the visible part or external nose and the nasal cavity which extends back into the skull.

The external nose is pyramidal in shape and is made up of cartilage supported by a bony framework. This framework is formed by the nasal bones and part of the frontal and maxillary bones. The cartilaginous and bony parts of the nose are connected together by continuous periosteum and perichondrium.

Skin covers the external nose, then extends into the vestibule or entrance of the nose where there are hairs or vibrissae.

At the base of the nose are the anterior nares separated in the midline by a strut of cartilage, the columella.

The nasal cavity is divided centrally by the nasal septum which is made up of cartilage and bone. Anteriorly is the septal cartilage, the posterior part of the septum is the vomer and part of the ethmoid bone.

The floor of the nose is the hard palate while the narrow roof is formed by the cribriform plate of the ethmoid bone and parts of the frontal and sphenoid bones. Posteriorly the nasal cavity connects with the nasal pharynx at the posterior choanae.

The lateral wall of the nose is formed mainly by the medial wall of the maxilla and the ethmoid bone. Situated on the lateral wall of the nasal cavity are three projections called the inferior, middle and superior turbinates. The inferior turbinate being a separate bone while the other two turbinates are part of the ethmoid bone.

Below each turbinate is a space called a meatus. Into the inferior meatus drains the nasolacrimal duct, into the middle meatus the maxillary, frontal and anterior ethmoid sinuses drain and into the superior meatus the posterior ethmoid sinuses drain. The sphenoid sinus drains above the superior meatus into the spheno-ethmoid recess.

Mucous membrane lines the nasal cavity and is of two types, respiratory or columnar ciliated epithelium and olfactory.

The ciliated epithelium lines the lower part of the nose and is closely adherent to the perichondrium and muco-periosteum. It has mucous and serous glands which produce up to 1 litre of mucous per day. This mucous covering is wafted along by the bending movement of the cilia and is swept into the post-nasal space and then swallowed.

Olfactory mucosa lines the upper part of the nose and can be distinguished by its yellow colour.

The nose has a rich bloody supply derived from branches of the external and internal carotid arteries. Situated on the anterior part of the septum is an aggregation of blood vessels called Little's Area.

Venous drainage is partially facial and partly intercranial so infection can spread upwards as a complication of nasal disease.

The nerve supply to the nose is from the Trigeminal nerve and sphenopalatine ganglion. Blocking of these nerves means that procedures on the nose can be carried out easily under local anaesthetic.

Functions of the nose

The nose is an airway, being the first part of the respiratory tract. Its respiratory functions are to warm, humidify and filter the inspired air. The turbinates increase the surface so that this can be carried out more efficiently.

The air is warmed by the rich blood supply and moistened by the secretions of the glands of the mucous membrane. Large particles are filtered by the vibrissae of the nose; small particles being caught by the sticky secretions in the nasal passages and carried along on the mucous covering by the action of the cilia.

The nose is the organ of smell, receiving the stimulus for the olfactory nerves. These are the first cranial nerves.

Odours dissolved in the secretions of the nose will stimulate the nerve endings of the olfactory mucosa. Nerve fibres pass through the cribriform plate of the ethmoid bone to the olfactory bulb where they synapse; from here the nerve fibres form the olfactory tracts to the temporal lobe of the brain.

The nasal cavity helps to give resonance to the voice.

The nose has certain reflex actions. Sneezing will occur in an attempt to expel foreign bodies from the nose. A smell of food will stimulate the flow of saliva and gastric juices. The nose is sensitive to temperature changes, a fall in temperature will increase the blood supply to the mucosa so that inspired air may be warmed.

Paranasal sinuses

The paranasal sinuses are air containing spaces which develop in the skull; they communicate with the nasal cavity by way of an opening or ostium and are lined by columnar ciliated epithelium which is continuous with the lining of the nose.

Fig 5 Lateral wall of nose

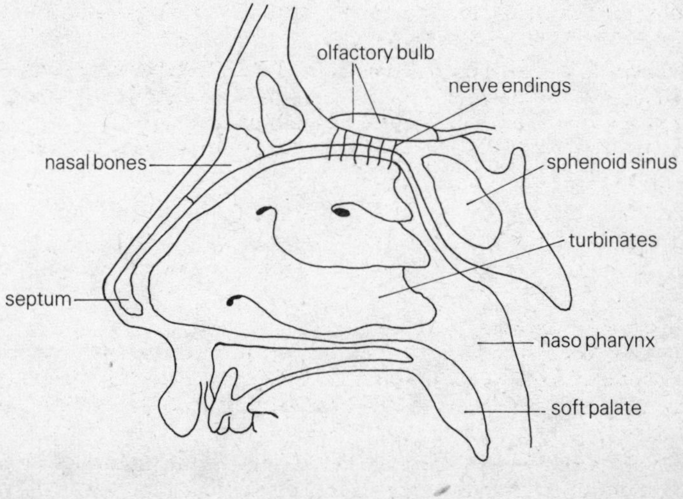

Maxillary sinus

The maxillary sinus or antrum occupies the body of the maxillary bone and is the largest of the sinuses having a capacity of about 15 mls. Although present at birth it does not reach its full size until after eruption of the second dentition. Triangular in shape with the apex into the zygoma and the base on the lateral wall of the nose.

The floor of the antrum is formed by the alvolar process and hard palate. Roots of some of the teeth may project into the antrum. In the child the floor lies above the level of the floor of the nose while in the adult it is $1\frac{1}{4}$ cm below. This must be taken into consideration when antrum washouts are performed.

The roof of the antrum is the thin floor of the orbit grooved by the infra-orbital nerve.

Anteriorly, is the cheek, whilst the nasolacrimal duct lies medially to the antrum. Nerves and blood vessels supplying the teeth run in the anterior and posterior walls.

The ostium of the antrum is set high in the medial wall and opens into the middle meatus. The position of the ostium means that mucous must be swept upwards by the cilia to drain the sinus; this can predispose to inefficient drainage and therefore the maxillary is the most commonly infected sinus; an accessory ostium may be present.

Fig 6 Nasal septum

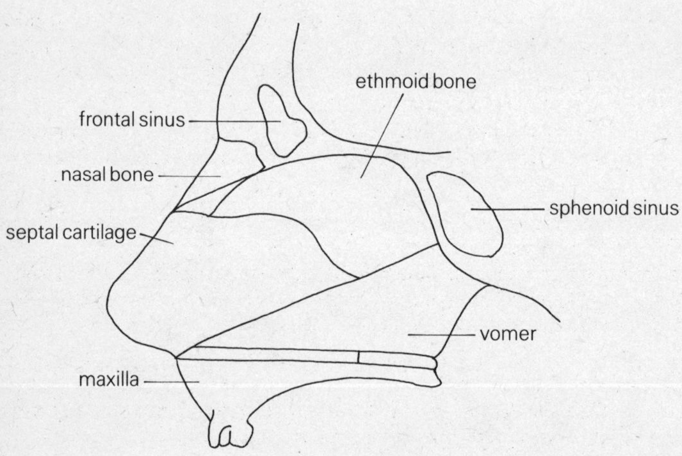

Fig 7 Nasal sinuses

Ethmoidal sinuses

The ethmoidal sinuses are a number of thin walled cells usually 7-15 which make up the main mass of the ethmoid bone. At birth there are 2 to 3 cells present.

The ethmoids are divided into an anterior and posterior group by the middle meatus. Drainage from the anterior group is into the middle meatus of the nose, whilst the posterior cells drain into the superior meatus.

Above the ethmoids lies the frontal sinus and the anterior cranial fossa. Inferiorly and laterally are the maxillary sinuses making approach to the ethmoids possible via a maxillary sinus.

The lacrimal sac and the optic nerve are related to the anterior and posterior ethmoid cells respectively.

Only a thin plate of bone, the lamina papyracea, separate the orbits from the ethmoids. The close proximity of the orbit means that disease of the ethmoids readily involves the eye.

Frontal sinus

The two frontal sinuses occupy a space in the frontal bone. They are separated by a septum and are often asymmetrical.

Absent at birth or only rudimentary they do not develop until about the age of 5-7 years.

The anterior wall is covered by the periosteum and skin of the forehead, whilst the posterior wall separates the sinuses from the frontal lobe of the brain. Below the sinuses are the orbits.

A long narrow frontonasal duct drains each sinus, passing through the anterior ethmoid cells to open into the middle meatus.

Sphenoidal sinus

The sphenoid sinus is present at birth and occupies the body of the sphenoid bone. It is divided usually into two by a septum which may be absent or oblique so that the right and left are rarely symmetrical.

Drainage of the sphenoid sinus is above the superior meatus into the spheno-ethmoidal recess.

The position of the sphenoidal sinuses within the skull means they are closely related to important intracranial structures.

Above lies the pituitary gland, optic chiasma, olfactory tract and frontal lobe of the brain. Laterally lies the optic nerve, carotid artery and cavernous sinus containing the III IV V VI cranial nerves.

Posterior is the basilar artery and brain-stem.

A surgical approach to the pituitary gland may be made via the sphenoidal sinus.

The function of the sinuses is uncertain.

Practice Questions

1. What constitutes the external nose?
2. What is the function of the vibrissae?
3. What is the columella?
4. What constitutes the nasal septum?
5. What structures can be seen on the lateral wall of the nose?
6. What is the function of the cilia?
7. What types of mucous membrane line the nose?
8. What is 'Little's Area'?
9. Where does the venous drainage of the nose go? How is this clinically important?
10. List the functions of the nose.
11. How do we smell?
12. What are the paranasal sinuses?
13. What is the capacity of the Maxillary Sinus?
14. When is the Maxillary Sinus fully developed?
15. What is the lamina papyracea?
16. What lies posterior to the frontal sinus?
17. Where is the sphenoid sinus situated?
18. What lies above the sphenoid sinus?
19. What drains into each part of the lateral wall of the nose?
20. How much mucous does the nose normally produce each day?

Answers

1. Cartilage supported by a framework of bone connected together by continuous periosteum and perichondrium covered by skin.
2. To filter large particles of dust from the inspired air.
3. A strut of cartilage separating the anterior nares.
4. Anteriorly — cartilage.
   Posteriorly — bone; the vomer and part of the ethmoid bone.
   Covered by mucoperichondrium and mucoperiosteum.
5. Superior, middle and inferior turbinates. Below them the superior, middle and inferior meatus.
6. By their bending movement to waft along the mucous covering into the postnasal space.
7. Respiratory or columna ciliated epithelium olfactory.
8. Aggregation of blood vessels on the anterior part of the nasal septum.
9. Partly facial, partly intercranial.
   Infection from the nose can be carried to the brain.

10. Part of the respiratory tract.
    Warms, moistens, so filters the air.
    Organ of smell.
    Helps give the voice resonance.
    Reflexes — sneezing. Smell of food stimulates salivation and gastric juices. Increases vascularity in low temperature.
11. Odours in solution stimulate the olfactory cells nerve endings. Nerves pass through the cribriform plate to the olfactory bulb via the olfactory tract to the temporal lobe of the brain.
12. Air containing cavities which develop in the skull and which communicate with the nose via their ostia.
13. Approximately 15mls.
14. When the second dentition is complete.
15. Thin bony partition between the ethmoid cells and the orbits.
16. The frontal lobe of the brain.
17. In the body of the sphenoid bone.
18. Pituitary gland, optic chiasma, olfactory tract and frontal lobe of the brain.
19. Inferior meatus — naso-lacrimal duct.
    Middle meatus — maxillary sinus
    — frontal sinus
    — anterior ethmoid cells.
    Superior meatus — posterior ethmoid cells.
    Spheno-ethmoidal recess — sphenoid sinus.
20. Up to 1 Litre per day.

Conditions of the nose

Patients presenting to the doctor with conditions of the nose or sinuses may complain of any of the following problems.

Nasal obstruction
This is the most common symptom of nasal disease.

Rhinorrhoea
Nasal discharge may be mucous mucopurulent and blood-stained.

Epistaxis
Bleeding from the nose.

Sneezing
Caused by irritation.

Anosmia
Loss of the sense of smell due either to damage to the olfactory area or secondary to nasal obstruction.

Headache: facial discomfort
Usually associated with sinus conditions.

After taking a history the doctor will look at the external nose and then examine the cavity using a nasal speculum. A view of the posterior part of the nasal cavity and a septum can be seen with a post-nasal mirror.

Nasal function may be disrupted by factors such as trauma, foreign bodies, infection, new growths, pathology outside the nose and psychological and environmental factors.

Nasal trauma

Nasal trauma may range from a simple fracture of the nasal bones and septum to part of the extensive facial injury which can occur, for example, after being propelled through the wind-screen of a car. These severe injuries however usually come within the sphere of reconstructive facial maxillary surgery. It is the simple fracture which is most often seen in the Ear, Nose and Throat Department. As these injuries invariably occur as a result of sport, violence or accident, the patients are usually fit young men or boys.

The patient will usually present with a deformed mobile nose, an associated swelling and bruising which may involve the eyes. There may be epistaxis and soft tissue lacerations.

An X-Ray is always taken as this could be used for legal evidence later. It is important to exclude other injuries such as face or head and look for evidence of cerebrospinal fluid rhinorrhoea which could indicate cribriform plate damage. Epistaxis must be treated and any facial lacerations cleaned and sutured if necessary. Prophylactic, antitetanus and antibiotics may be given.

The most opportune time for a nasal fracture to be reduced is immediately after injury before swelling can occur. However, as this is unlikely to happen, the swelling is usually present by the time the patient is seen. Operation must therefore wait until the oedema has subsided a few days later. Under a general anaesthetic the nasal bones and septum are re-positioned. The nose is usually packed for 24 hours and a plaster of paris splint applied to the outside of the nose. This splint is kept on for about a week and is then worn at night for about another week.

Hospitalisation is usually very short and the patients are warned to avoid further injury. However, this is often disregarded.

An injury of the nose can result in a deviated septum and deformities of the external nose.

Foreign bodies

Some small children from time to time like to put objects, such as beads, buttons or paper up their noses.

The foreign body may be expelled by the initial attack of sneezing which the irritation provokes. Parents may be aware of what the child has done and seek advice. Epistaxis can occur as a result of trauma from the foreign body.

Sometimes the foreign body will remain in the nose until the child is found to have a unilateral discharge. When there is infection present discharge will become offensive and green.

Treatment is removal using a good light and the right instruments. A round object such as a bead is removed by passing a blunt hook behind it; hooking it forward. Other foreign bodies may be picked out with nasal forceps.

With a co-operative child this may be performed in the Out-Patient Department. Sometimes a general anaesthetic is necessary to ensure a quiet child.

The potential danger of a nasal foreign body is the risk of it going into the post-nasal space and then being inhaled, trauma, epistaxis and infection. Trauma, bleeding and the possibility of being pushed post-nasally can occur as a result of attempting removal in a struggling child.

Deviated septum

The nasal cavity is divided into two by the septum. These are rarely symmetrical. Normally this does not cause any problem unless the septum is grossly deviated.

A septum may become deviated either during development and growth of the face, or as a result of injury.

The deviation may be to one side or S shaped and spurs may form as a result of thickening of the tissue. When a deviation obstructs one side of the nose and widens the other, the mucosa of the turbinate of the wide side may hypertrophy to compensate.

The patient with a deviated septum will always complain of nasal obstruction. Headaches can occur from poor aeration of the sinuses. Blockage of the ostia can predispose to sinusitis. The sense of smell is usually not impaired unless the deviation is a large one.

Traditionally the operation for a deviated septum has been submucous resection (S.M.R.). This has now been replaced in many instances by septoplasty.

Submucous resection

An incision is made in the mucosa on one side of the septum. The mucosa is then elevated from the septal cartilage and bone on both sides.

After removal of as much of the cartilage and bone as is necessary the two layers of the mucosa lie together and may be sutured. Splints are sometimes placed either side of the septum and the nose will be packed.

Post-operative care is as for all nasal surgery.

Specific complications which can occur after septal surgery:
Septal Haematoma — probably the most common complication.
Septal Abscess — following infection of a haematoma.
Septal Perforation — can occur particularly when the mucosa is perforated opposite the incision.
Nasal Deformity — can occur when too much septum has been removed.

For this reason S.M.R. is not performed before the nose has fully developed.

Septoplasty
This is a similar procedure to S.M.R. except that instead of removing the deviated part of the septum it is re-positioned.

After septal surgery the patient is advised that the full benefit of the operation will not be felt for a few weeks until the oedema has subsided.

Septal haematoma and abscess
A septal haematoma is a collection of blood between the mucoperichondrium and the cartilge of the nasal septum and appears as a red swelling blocking the nose.

It can occur as a result of trauma, a complication of septal surgery, or associated with an acute infection usually virol.

A small haematoma may be treated with antibiotics and possible aspiration but a large one must be incised and drained. Under a general anaesthetic an incision is made in Little's Area the clot sucked out and a drain, such as corrugated tubing or ribbon gauze left in situ and the nose packed. Antibiotics must be given to prevent infection and abscess formation.

A septal abscess is usually secondary to a haematoma though it can also occur spontaneously after infection. Swelling of the septum obstructs the nose, the patient is pyrexial and complains of a headache and severe throbbing pain.

Treatment is incision, drainage and antibiotics.

A septal haematoma and abscess can cut off the blood supply to the cartilage causing it to necrosis. This may lead to septal perforation or nasal deformity. With antibiotics the risk of intracranial complications is rare.

Nasal infections
Nasal infections may be acute or chronic.

Furunculosis
This is an acute staphylococcus infection of the vibrissae of the nasal vestibule.

The inflammation causes a tense red painful swelling usually at the tip of the nose. Antibiotics are prescribed and the furuncle allowed to point and burst when ready. Squeezing and incision must be avoided because of risk of spreading infection. Infection, via the venous drainage has been known to cause cavernous sinus thrombosis.

With recurrent furunculosis it is advisable to carry out bacteriological examinations and test the patients' urine as diabetes may be an underlying factor.

Acute rhinitis

Acute rhinitis or coryza is, of course, the common cold with which everyone is very familiar. It is probably viral in origin with secondary bacterial infection.

Chronic rhinitis

In this condition the patient tends to complain of 'catarrh' by which they usually mean nasal discharge and a stuffy nose.

There are many factors which are thought to predispose or contribute to the chronic inflammatory process.

These may be:

Infection — repeated attacks of acute rhinitis or nearby infection such as sinusitis.
Irritants — from atmospheric pollution such as dust, fumes, industrial chemicals.
Environmental — like overcrowding, central heating.
Life Style — smoking, alcohol, lack of exercise.
Diet — dietary imbalance.
Endocrine — disorders especially of thyroid.
Iatrogenic — over use of nasal drops or sprays can be detrimental to the nasal mucosa.
Obstruction — caused by, for example, septal defects.
Drugs — a side effect of some drugs e.g. the contraceptive pill.
Vasomotor rhinitis
Here there are vascular changes due to the imbalance of the autonomic nervous supply to the mucosa.
Psychological
Emotional or stressful states.
Nasal allergy

The patient with chronic rhinitis complains of a stuffy nose with a nasal discharge. A post-nasal drip will give a tendency to keep clearing the throat. There may be nasal irritation, headaches and anosmia.

On examination the nasal mucosa is seen to be swollen and congested with strands of mucopurulent secretion. At other times pale and oedematious.

The conditions may progress to hypertrophic rhinitis when permanent changes have taken place; then the mucosa has become thickened and hypertrophied, the turbinates enlarged with a mulberry like appearance. Nasal polyps may be seen.

Investigations are carried out to find a possible cause, or predisposing factor. This may then be treated.

Advice can be given on changes in life style such as not smoking, cutting down on alcohol, having more fresh air and exercise.

Decongestive nasal drops may be given for a limited period only to avoid further damage to the mucosa.

Surgery may be undertaken to reduce congestion and increase the space in the nasal cavity.

The enlarged ends of the inferior turbinates may be amputated.

Submucosal diathermy consists of putting a diathermy needle under the mucosa of the turbinate. The resulting scar will contract and reduce the size of the turbinate.

A deviated septum may be corrected with an S.M.R. or septoplasty.

Epistaxis

Epistaxis, or bleeding from the nose is not a disease itself, but a symptom of disease.

Causes of epistaxis are usually grouped as local or general and include.

Local Causes

Spontaneous

This is probably due to congested blood-vessels which bleed on slight trauma such as picking. Commonly from Little's Area.

Trauma

Trauma may be slight such as picking or a foreign body, or a more serious injury inflicted by a blow or accident.

Infection

Associated with acute or chronic rhinitis.

Tumours

Benign e.g. Haemangioma
Malignant e.g. Carcinoma

Post-operatively

After nose and sinus surgery.

GENERAL CAUSES

Hypertension
Associated with conditions such as arterial disease.

Raised venous pressure
e.g. congestive cardiac failure

Blood disorders
e.g. Leukaemia.

Clotting disorders
e.g. Haemophilia.

Febrile conditions
e.g. Influenza, Measles.

Drug induced
e.g. anticoagulant therapy.

Associated with menstruation

The incidence of epistaxis is seen mainly in children and the middle to elderly age group. In children the bleeding is usually spontaneous and may readily be seen coming from Little's Area. Hypertension is commonly the cause in the older age groups and tends to be less easily visible as it often occurs from further back in the nose.

Blood loss may vary from a few drops to a severe life threatening haemorrhage.

The principles of treatment and care of a patient with epistaxis are to:

Control the bleeding and treat any shock.
Estimate the blood loss and replace.
Investigate and treat the cause, the priorities depending upon the severity of the bleed and the condition of the patient.

Patients may receive treatment in the Out-Patient Department and then are able to go home, others require emergency admission.

The patient is usually sat up, unless shocked, in which case they are best in a recovery position to protect the airway.

First-aid treatment for an epistaxis can be carried out by a nurse. The patient is sat with their head forward over a bowl; the nostrils are firmly pinched and an ice pack may be put on the bridge of the nose. Clothes should be protected. The doctor will examine the nose, remove any clots with forceps or suction and spray with a local anaesthetic.

Providing the bleeding spot can be seen, it may be cauterised with either a chemical such as silver-nitrate or trichloracetic acid, or by use of the galvic electric cautery under a local anaesthetic. The electric cautery will never be used on a child without a general anaesthetic. Alternatively the nose will be packed using possibly ribbon gauze impregnated with a substance such as B.I.P.P. (bismuth iodoform paraffin paste) a gauze packed glove finger, or an inflatable balloon type pack.

Post-nasal packs may be inserted if the bleeding is far back. A post-nasal pack is a gauze pad with three strings attached. A fine catheter is slid along the floor of each nostril into the pharynx and removed from the mouth with forceps. A string of the pack is attached to each catheter which are then withdrawn pulling the pack into the post-nasal space. The two strings are tied over some padding on the columella. The third string is attached loosely on to the cheek until it is needed for removing the pack.

Antibiotic cover is usually given when a nasal pack is being left in for a time.

Blood will be taken for Hb. X match and full blood picture.

An intravenous infusion may be set up.

Nursing care of patients with epistaxis

The Nurse will assess the patient, identify the problems and potential problems and plan the care to meet the needs of the individual patient.

It is usual for a patient with a severe epistaxis to be at bed rest until the pack is removed. Therefore, the possible complications of bed rest should be prevented.

The patient will have suffered a blood loss and therefore may have anaemia, fluid and electrolyte imbalance. An intravenous infusion or transfusion may be in progress and iron supplements prescribed. Oral fluid will be encouraged and a fluid balance chart maintained. Pulse and blood presure will be monitored.

A nasal pack in situ will mean mouth breathing, a dry mouth and anosmia. Attention must therefore be given to oral care.

Limited mobility will mean the patient will need help with hygiene. Appropriate pressure area care given and leg movement and breathing exercises encouraged.

There will probably be loss of appetite due to the difficulty of eating and mouth breathing and the anosmia. Small nutritious meals can be supplemented with high calorie drinks, if necessary.

Constipation and straining should be avoided, their diet should contain fibre and aperients given when needed. Urinary output will be monitored.

Patients are usually anxious and afraid after a bleed, therefore explanation and reassurance are needed to allay fears. A mild sedative may be given to ensure rest.

Any treatment which the patient may already be on is incorporated into the care.

After removal of the nasal packs, the patient is mobilised gradually and the care adapted to the patient's changing needs.

Packing a nose does not guarantee the bleeding is controlled. Oozing can occur around a pack. After removal the patient may again bleed and need re-packing. Nose blowing is advised against for a while.

Occasionally surgical intervention is necessary for a severe or persistent epistaxis and will involve ligation of the blood-vessel which is causing the bleeding. This may be the anterior ethmoid artery using an incision near the inner canthus of the eye, the maxillary artery via a Caldwell-Luc approach or the eternal carotid in the neck.

Investigations should always be carried out to find the cause of the epistaxis if it is not known. Referral may be made to a Physician or Haematologist, either while in Hospital, or from the patient's General Practitioner.

Nasal allergy

This is the term used to describe the nasal symptoms which are produced when a sensitised individual is exposed to a specific foreign protein or allergen.

On exposure to specific allergens an atopic individual will produce quantities of immunoglobulin 1gE. These will attach themselves to the mast cells in the nasal mucosa.

Later exposure will cause a binding of the antigen and the 1gE on the mast cell surface. The cell membrane will become more permeable and release its granules of histamine and similar substances. These will produce the characteristic picture of nasal allergy:

Nasal irritation and paroxysmal sneezing.

Rhinorrhoea with clear watery secretions containing eosinophils.

The eyes can be affected with conjunctival injection, soreness and profuse lacrimation.

The mucosa which is oedematious looks pale or bluish in colour.

The oedematious mucosa will lead to nasal obstruction and commonly nasal polypi formation.

Symptoms may fluctuate considerably over a period of time. Allergy may be seasonal or perennial.

For some people the condition lasts only during the summer months when the pollen count is raised and is then commonly known as hay fever. Others suffer throughout the year when the condition is then perennial.

Investigations

A careful history should be taken to try and identify any predisposing causes and possible allergens.

There may be a family history of nasal allergy or associated conditions such as asthma and eczema; psychological factors may be present. Other possible predisposing causes can be endocrine changes such as those which occur at puberty or the menopause, environmental, or infection which may cause further irritation to an already sensitive area.

Skin tests are done to identify possible allergens. Commercially prepared test solutions of common allergens are used. Small quantities of the solutions are introduced under the skin of the forearm. A wheel indicates a positive reaction. The patient should be watched in case any allergic reaction either local or systemic occurs. Piriton or hydrocortisone may be given.

The most common allergens are the house dust mite, pollen feathers and animal danders. Many people are allergic to more than one allergen.

Treatment

The patient is advised to try and avoid contact with the allergens though this is not always easy.

Advice is given on environmental control such as methods of cleaning.

A course of desensitisation injections may be given before the onset of the pollen season for hay fever sufferers. After each injection the patient must be closely observed for any sign of an adverse reaction. This may vary from a local erythema to a serious complication such as bronchospasm laryngeal oedema or anaphylactic shock. Drugs such as adrenaline, hydrocortisone aminophylline and supportive measures should always be available.

Anti-histamine helps the symptoms but has troublesome side effects.

The drug sodium chromoglycate is used as a spray prophylactically. It appears to prevent the release of the cell granules by stabilising the mast cell membrane.

Systemic steroids may be used, but only for a limited period because of adverse side effects. Tropical steroids can also be used.

Surgery, to improve the nasal airway, such as S.M.R. submucosal diathermy, or nasal polypectomy, may be undertaken.

Treatment of any predisposing causes.

Allergic rhinitis occurs frequently in children and young adults. Seasonal allergy usually coincides with examination time and so places them under additional strain. Symptomatic treatment can therefore be a great help to them. Nasal allergy is frequently associated with secretory otitis media in children.

Cocaine

Cocaine can be used for topical application in the nose, either in the form of cocaine solution 5% and 10% with equal parts of adrenaline 1:1,000 or as cocaine paste. These may be used for:

Out-Patient procedures
Prior to nasal surgery
Surgery under local anaesthetic

The drugs may be sprayed into the nose or applied either on ribbon gauze or cotton-wool wrapped on to wool carriers.

Cocaine acts as a local anaesthetic and because of its effect on the sympathetic nervous system promotes vasoconstriction. Adrenaline also provides vasoconstriction and enhances the effect of the cocaine.

Individuals vary in their sensitivity to cocaine and therefore some people may experience side effects. Because of this no patient should be left unobserved once the drugs are *in situ*.

A sensitive patient may experience nausea, faintness and confusion. They will become pale and sweating with a tachycardia and a falling blood pressure. Severe reaction, though rare, could progress to convulsions and death from respiratory arrest.

Should a patient show any indication of adverse effects the cocaine should immediately be removed, the Medical Staff informed and the patient put in a head down position and kept warm.

A reaction can be precipitated by lack of food, so unless the patient is having a general anaesthetic, food should not be withheld. Removal of the cocaine and a glucose drink is usually sufficient to improve the patient's condition. In severe cases it may be necessary for a doctor to administer drugs such as diazepan.

It is very important that all members of the Nursing Staff are aware of potential problems when cocaine is being used.

Many doctors, because of the risk of possible reaction in a sensitive patient, prefer to use other forms of local anaesthetic such as solution of lignocaine with adrenaline.

Care of patients having nasal surgery

Patients for nasal surgery are usually admitted the day before operation and routine pre-operative preparation is carried out. Some Surgeons may request removal of a moustache in a male patient to help prevent possible post-operative infection.

Prior to surgery the nose may be packed with ribbon gauze which has been rung out in a local anaesthetic such as cocaine and adrenaline or lignocaine with adrenaline. This is to promote vasoconstriction and so increase haemostasis.

After surgery there is usually a nasal pack *in situ* which should be secured externally to prevent it falling out or slipping post-nasally. The packs may possibly be, for example, impregnated, ribbon gauze, vaseline gauze, or glove fingers packed with ribbon gauze. A nasal bolster which is a piece of folded gauze is taped under the nose to absorb any oozing; this can be renewed as necessary.

In the immediate post-operative period, the care of the airway is of first priority, as there is the additional risk of blood trickling down from the post-nasal space. Also the presence of the pack will mean the patient can only mouth breath and there is always the possible risk of the end of a ribbon gauze pack slipping down into the airway.

When the patient is fully conscious and the pulse and blood pressure satisfactory they may be propped up as this will lessen venous congestion.

The patient is made clean and comfortable and oral fluids may be started. Care should be taken to avoid scalding by not giving hot drinks to patients who have had a local anaesthetic until sensation has returned.

The patient is able to mobilise gradually next day.

Should the end of the pack slip down into the pharynx and is uncomfortable for the patient, it can be shortened. However a loop of the pack must not be cut or a piece may be left in when the pack is removed.

Usually the pack is removed 24-48 hours post-operatively by a nurse. It is explained to the patient that they should remain resting for a while after the procedure. The packs are removed gently and carefully with nasal dressing forceps, or a gloved hand. With packed glove fingers the ribbon gauze is removed first. Some bleeding will inevitably follow removal of the pack so the patient must rest and an ice pack may be applied to the nose. The patient can mobilise when the bleeding has stopped.

Following operations such as S.M.R. or nasal polypectomy, steam inhalations and decongestant nasal drops such as ephedrine may be prescribed. These will be commenced a few hours after the pack is removed and given 4 hourly.

Crusting may occur after septal surgery. The crusts can be removed by the medical or trained nursing staff.

After removal of the packs patients are advised not to blow their noses for some time, even after going home; the time being dependent on the operation.

Most patients will be self-caring the day after nasal surgery and recovery is usually quick and uneventful.

However, possible complications should always be observed for and any bleeding, swelling, pain, pyrexia, headache, drowsiness or eye problems such as diplopia, should be reported. It is especially important to watch out for any indication of infection because the risk of infection, leading to thrombosis of the cavernous sinus, should not be overlooked.

Stay in hospital after nasal surgery is usually only a few days and then the patient will be followed up in the Out-Patients Department.

Practice Questions

1. Explain the terms:
   a Rhinorrhoea
   b Anosmia
   c Vasomotor Rhinitis
   d Hay Fever
   e Immunoglobulin 1 gE
2. When may the following drugs be used in Ear, Nose and Throat?
   a Cocaine
   b Adrenaline
   c Ephedrine
   d Sodium Chromoglycate
3. What are the possible complications of a:
   a Fractured Nose
   b Nasal foreign body
   c S.M.R.
   d Septal Haematoma
4. List possible predisposing causes of chronic rhinitis.
5. Clear rhinorrhoea containing eosinophiles usually indicates:
   a Nasal allergy
   b Foreign body
   c Coryza
   d Sinusitis
6. The most likely cause of perennial allergic rhinitis is:
   a Milk
   b Detergent
   c Pollen
   d House dust mite
7. Epistaxis is most likely to arise from the:
   a Maxillary sinuses
   b Floor of the nose
   c Nasal septum
   d Inferior turbinate
8. A nasal furuncule will be treated by:
   a Incision
   b Antibiotics

c Aspiration
d Antibiotics + incision

9. David Johnson aged 28 is admitted for S.M.R. under local anaesthetic.

A The operation is performed for:
a Fractured Nose
b Deviated Septum
c Septal Haematoma
d Septal Perforation

B The patient will most likely have sought advice for:
a Nasal obstruction
b Nasal deformity
c Rhinorrhoea
d Anosmia

C Mr Johnson's nose was packed with cocaine 10% and adrenaline 1:1,000 before the operation. He was then:
a told not to worry if he felt unwell
b allowed to rest quietly alone
c observed for any adverse effects
d sat propped up with pillows

D A Nurse was instructed that if the patient showed any signs of shock she must first:
a report to the doctor
b give the patient a glucose drink
c get an extra blanket
d take out the pack

E After the operation Mr Johnson said he was thirsty so he was:
a given a hot drink
b given a cold drink
c given nothing to drink
d given a mouthwash

F Inhalation and nasal drops were prescribed and were commenced:
a morning after operation
b immediately after removal of the nasal pack
c a few hours after removal of the nasal pack
d the second post-operative day

G On discharge Mr Johnson was aware that:
a he could now smell normally
b his nose was a different shape
c he had a clear airway
d his airway would improve as the swelling subsided

10. Thomas Williams aged 67 known to be hypertensive is admitted to the Ward from the Out-Patients Department with a fairly severe epistaxis. A post-nasal and anterior pack are *in situ*.

Using a problem solving approach plan Mr Williams' care until after the pack is removed. Give reason for the planned care.

Answers

1. **a** Rhinorrhoea — nasal discharge.
   b Anosmia — loss of the sense of smell.
   c Vasomotor rhinitis — a chronic inflammatory condition of the nose where there are vascular changes due to the imbalance of the autonomic nerve supply to the mucosa.
   d Hay fever — seasonal allergic rhinitis commonly caused by pollen occurring in the summer months.
   e Immunoglobulin 1 gE — is produced by an atopic individual when exposed to a specific allergen. They attach themselves to the mast cells and will bind with a specific allergen causing the release of histamine and similar substances.
2. **a** Cocaine — used as a local anaesthetic and to promote vasoconstriction; commonly used for nasal procedures.
   b Adrenaline — used for its vasoconstrictive properties enhances the action of cocaine.
   c Ephedrine — used as decongestive nasal drops.
   d Sodium chromoglycate — used propholactically for allergic rhinitis — stabilises the mast cell membrane.
3. **a** Possible:
   Epistaxis
   C.S.F. rhinorrhoea
   Deviated Septum
   Deformity of external nose
   b Nasal trauma
   Epistaxis
   Rhinorrhoea
   Infection
   Going through post-nasal space and being inhaled
   c Septal Haematoma
   Septal Abscession
   Septal Perforation
   Nasal Deformity
   Infection
   d Septal Abscess
   Necrosis of Cartilage
   Deformity
   Spread of Infection
4.
   Infection
   Irritants

Environmental
Excess alcohol and smoking
Dietary imbalance
Endocrine
Over use of nose drops
Nasal obstruction
Drug side effects
Vasomotor rhinitis
Emotion, stress
Nasal allergy

5. **a**
6. **d**
7. **c**
8. **b**
9. *A* **b**
   B **a**
   C **c**
   D **d**
   E **b**
   F **c**
   G **d**
10. See overleaf

10. EPISTAXIS CARE PLAN

Problems	*Care Plan*	*Reason/Significance*
Blood loss	Monitor pulse & blood pressure	Monitor condition
	Care of i/v infusion/transfusion	— Replace fluid-electrolytes
	Encourage oral fluids	— Maintain hydration
	Monitor fluid balance	
Anaemia	Iron supplements if ordered	— Correct anaemia
Risk of further bleeding	— Observe for bleeding:— — round pack — after removal	— Monitor
Hypertension	— Hypertensive drugs as prescribed	Lower blood pressure
Nasal pack *in situ*	— Change guaze pad under nose as necessary	— Maintain nasal hygiene
	— Remove pack when ordered	— Prevent discomfort
Mouth breathing	— Oral care — mouth washes	— Keep mouth clean and comfortable
Possible loss of appetite due to pack and anosmia	Small meals	
	Supplement with high calorie drinks	Maintain nutrition
Limited mobility	— Physiotherapy to limbs and chest	Prevent the complications of bedrest
due to bedrest	— Encourage limb movements and breathing exercises	
	— Care of pressure areas	
Not able to maintain	— Assist with hygiene, oral hygiene	Maintain hygiene and patient's comfort
own hygiene	Gradual ambulation & independence	— Encourage independence
	Independence when packs are removed and bleeding controlled	
Risk of constipation	— Appropriate diet	Prevent constipation and straining
	— aperients if needed	
Anxiety	— Sedatives if ordered	
	— Communication with patient	Relieve anxiety
	— Identify any specific problems	promote rest
	— Refer to other discipline if appropriate e.g. Medical Social Worker	

Sinusitis

Sinusitis — inflammation of the paranasal sinuses, may be acute or chronic.

Acute sinusitis

Acute sinusitis may be caused by a bacterial infection, for example streptococci, staphlococci, or viral infection.
— most commonly a complication of acute rhinitis
— can occur after dental infection or extraction
— as a result of trauma or foreign body
— following swimming or diving.

Predisposing factors are anything which prevents drainage of the sinuses such as a deviated septum or nasal polypi.

Infection spreads into the sinus from the nose causing the mucous membrane to become inflamed, oedematous and produce excess mucous. The ostium becomes blocked and the cilia action impaired. Infection causes pus formation which further damages the cilia. Secretions are unable to drain into the nose. Stagnation of secretions result in a build up of pressure in the surrounding tissues causing pain and discomfort.

Acute maxillary sinusitis

This is the most commonly infected of the sinuses and may occur alone or with infection of the other sinuses.

The patient usually has a history of a recent cold, flu, or sometimes dental infection. They complain of headache, facial discomfort, a blocked nose, feeling ill and are pyrexial.

The nasal mucosa is inflamed and if the ostium is open, pus can be seen in the middle meatus.

A nasal swab will be taken for culture and sensitivity and a sinus X ray will show haziness and probably a fluid level.

Treatment

Treatment will be antibiotics, probably penicillin unless the swab culture indicates otherwise.

Decongestant nasal drops and steam inhalations will facilitate drainage from the ostium.

Analgesic for relief of pain.

Bed rest and extra fluids until the temperature has returned to normal.

Should the symptoms not resolve within a day or two an antrum washout may be carried out. This is never performed in the acute stage until after the antibiotics have been given because of the risk of introducing infection into the bone. A specimen of the washout will be sent for culture and sensitivity.

Complications
This may spread infection to the other sinuses, middle ear, throat or the chest.

Acute frontal sinusitis
This is predisposed to by anything which causes blockage of the long frontonasal duct.

Clinical features are similar to those of maxillary sinusitis.

The patient feels ill, complains of pain over the eyes and has a headache which is worse in the morning and improves during the afternoon.

Pressure on the floor of the sinus is painful.

An X ray will show opacity of the sinus and usually involvement of the ethmoids and maxillary sinus.

Due to the close proximity of the eye, the upper eyelid may be oedematous.

Treatment
This is the same as for maxillary sinusitis, antibiotics, inhalations, nasal drops, analgesic and care of a pyrexial patient. However, because of the possible risk of eye and intracranial complications, the patients will need to be admitted to hospital.

In some cases surgical drainage of the sinus may be necessary. A hole is trephined below the eyebrow into the floor of the sinus. A drainage tube *in situ* may be used for irrigation of the sinus.

Ethmoid Sinusitis
Acute ethmoid sinusitis usually occurs with maxillary and frontal.

The pain is between the eyes and nasal discharge is seen in the middle and superior meatus.

In a child there may be redness and swelling below the inner canthus of the eye.

Treatment
This is the same as for maxillary sinusitis with appropriate eye care, if necessary.

Sphenoidal sinusitis
Acute sphenoidal sinusitis is rare and usually occurs as part of a panasinusitis. The patient complains of severe headache and a post-nasal drip may be seen when the nose is examined with a post-nasal mirror.

Treatment
Again this is the treatment of the associated maxillary sinusitis.

The sphenoid sinus may be washed out with a sphenoid sinus canula. Due to its position within the skull there is a risk of intercranial spread of infection.

Chronic Sinusitis
This is chronic inflammation of the sinus mucosa which may also involve the surrounding bone. The mucosa will undergo permanent changes.

Causes
The two main causal factors are probably infection and allergy. They may occur together.

With recurrent attacks of acute infection the healing process will cause scarring and narrowing of the ostia and prevent drainage and aeration of the sinuses.

An allergic reaction will result in oedema and thickening of the mucosa, again with blockage of the ostia.

Other predisposing causes may be:

Inadequate treatment of the acute attacks.
Poor resistance of the patient often associated with an unbalanced diet.
Atmospheric pollution which means this condition is commonly associated with industrial areas.

Whatever the cause the mucosa becomes thickened and often polypoidal. The ostium is blocked leading to stagnation of secretions and cilia drainage. Secondary infection may then occur.

Clinical features
The symptoms tend to be vague unless an acute attack occurs on top of the chronic situation, otherwise the patient will complain of nasal-obstruction, a mucopurulent nasal discharge or post-nasal drip. The latter can cause a secondary pharyngitis or laryngitis.

Treatment
This is usually surgical to:

Remove the infection
Restore drainage
Improve the nasal airway.

Chronic Maxillary Sinusitis
This may also be associated with dental infections.

Treatment
At first this will probably be repeated antrum washouts.

Antrum washouts

This procedure may be performed in the ward, Out-Patients Department or Theatre under either local or general anaesthetic.

A Tilley Lichtwitz trocar and cannula is introduced into the maxillary sinus through the inferior meatus. The trocar is removed and the sinus washed out with sterile water, or saline via the cannula using a syringe.

Fluid can go into the soft tissues causing swelling round the eye if the cannula is not correctly placed. For this reason the eyes are left uncovered and observed when an antrum washout is performed in Theatre. The washout may be sent for culture and sensitivity.

Should the condition not improve an intranasal antrostomy may be done, or a Caldwell-Luc operation.

Intranasal Antrostomy

An opening or antrostomy is made from the nose into the sinus under the inferior meatus to improve drainage and aeration of the sinus.

The sinus can be washed out when necessary using only a curved blunt cannula through the new ostium. If this does not improve the condition the next stage will be a Caldwell-Luc operation.

Caldwell-Luc operation or radical antrostomy

The incision is made in the upper gum in the canine fossa and a hole made through to the antrum the antral mucosa is removed. An intranasal antrostomy is made into the nose in the inferior meatus and the nasal mucosa reflected through this opening.

Regeneration of the antrum mucosa should take place from the nose through to the antrum. The gum incision is usually sutured with catgut.

The new antrostomy provides improved drainage and facilitates antrum washouts should they be necessary.

Care must be taken during this operation not to damage the infra-orbital nerve which is in the roof of the sinus.

The Caldwell-Luc approach to the sinus may also be used to:

Remove a foreign body.

Explore where a neoplasm is suspected.

Clip the maxillary artery for epistaxis.

After a blow-out fracture of the maxilla when the orbital muscles have prolapsed downwards, the sinus is packed after returning the orbital contents.

Chronic frontal sinusitis

The patient with chronic frontal sinusitis will complain of pain and headache.

Treatment

Conservative treatment will usually be tried first. Any co-existing maxillary or ethmoidal infection is treated. Also any condition such as a deviated septum which may be impairing drainage of the frontonasal duct must be treated.

At times however more radical surgery has to be considered. The aim of the surgery is to remove infection, establish better drainage and occasionally to obliterate the sinus.

Frontal sinus exploration

An incision is made medial to the orbit. The floor of the sinus is removed, infected mucosa and any diseased ethmoid cells removed and the frontonasal duct is enlarged. This is usually kept patent by inserting a wide bore tube which is cut short and remains inside the nose for several weeks. The incision is sutured with fine silk to give a good cosmetic scar.

Macbeth's operation

The operation is performed to explore and obliterate the frontal sinus. An incision is made from ear to ear above the hairline and the scalp reflected down to the eyebrows. Good access can be obtained to both the sinuses by raising the anterior wall as a bone flap. Diseased tissue is removed, drainage provided into the nose and the blood clot will fibrose obliterating the sinus. This operation, though a fairly major procedure, gives a good cosmetic result once the hair has regrown, because the incision is above the hairline.

Chronic ethmoidal sinusitis

This occurs alongside chronic infection in the other sinuses and is associated with recurrent nasal polypi formation.

Nasal polypi

They commonly arise from the ethmoid sinuses and hang in the nasal cavity causing a nasal obstruction.

The mucosa of the turbinates and the antrum can also become polypoidal.

Occasionally a single antral polypi may extrude through the ostia and hang in the post-nasal space. This is known as an antrochoanal polypi.

Treatment of chronic ethmoid disease may be:

— nasal polypectomy
— intranasal ethmoidectomy
— external ethmoidectomy.

Nasal polypectomy
Nasal polypi may be removed under a local or general anaesthetic using a nasal snare and forceps. The nose may then be packed depending on the amount of blood loss. Unfortunately nasal polypi do tend to recur.

Intranasal ethmoidectomy
The bony partitions between the ethmoid cells are broken down following removal of the polypi and diseased mucosa. As this is done intranasally, using a speculum, great care must be taken not to damage nearby structures such as the eye muscles, cribriform plate or the orbit.

External ethmoidectomy
An incision is made medial to the orbit. This gives a direct approach to the ethmoid cells which can be removed.

Some surgical procedures have been designed to give an approach to more than one of the sinuses. One example of this is the Horgan operation.

Transantral ethmoidectomy or Horgan operation
This operation allows access to the antrum and the ethmoids.

A Caldwell-Luc operation is performed and the ethmoids approached through an incision in the medial wall of the sinus.

Sinusitis in children
In the child sinusitis tends to be chronic rather than acute, the antrum and ethmoids being the most common site of infection.

Acute maxillary sinusitis
Uncommon in children. This would present in a similar way as in the adult, though there may also be some oedema of the cheek.

Treatment
This would be bed rest, antibiotics and nasal decongestants.

Acute ethmoidal sinusitis
Sometimes seen in children, associated with maxillary infection and treated in the same way. Redness and swelling of the inner corner of the eye may occur requiring surgical drainage when the abscess points. An antrum washout will be done under a general anaesthetic.

Chronic maxillary sinusitis
This is common in children giving rise to a mucopurulent discharge, mouth breathing, cough and possible ear infections.

It may start as a complication of a condition such as a cold, measles, tonsillitis, dental infection or the presence of a foreign body. Resolution may be prevented by certain predisposing factors such as:

— enlarged adenoids
— septic tonsils
— chest infections
— nasal allergy
— presence of a foreign body
— low physical resistance to infection
— environmental factors such as poor social conditions.

Treatment

This will include treatment of any associated conditions such as allergy or infection, or general poor health. Surgical treatment could include:

— removal of the tonsils and adenoids
— antrum washout under a general anaesthetic
— polythene tubing may be left in the sinus to provide a means of irrigation
— intranasal antrostomy can be performed to improve drainage
— should an antrochoanal polypi be present it can be removed
— a Caldwell-Luc operation is avoided, because of risk to the dentition.

Care of patients with acute sinusitis

This patient has an acute infection and therefore the nursing care will initially be that of a pyrexia patient at bed rest.

The patient will need to be kept cool and the temperature and pulse monitored four hourly.

Assistance will be needed with hygiene and oral care though they will usually be allowed to get up to the toilet.

Fluids are encouraged and diet taken as they feel able.

Antibiotics are administered as prescribed and analgesics given for pain.

Steam inhalations and decongestant nasal drops are given as ordered.

Eye care and the instillation of drops may be needed should the eye be involved.

Possible complications and the spread of infection should be observed for. Any indication that the infection may have spread to the other sinuses, respiratory tract, middle ear, the orbit, into the bone, or intracranially, should be reported.

The patient usually mobilises when the acute symptoms have subsided.

Care of the patient after having surgery of the nasal sinuses

The care of the patient having surgery to the nasal sinuses is similar to that for patients having nasal surgery, although it may vary according to the particular operation.

Pre-operative preparation
This may include:

X ray of the sinuses.
Hb and electrolyte estimation.
Blood cross-matched if more extensive surgery undertaken.
Macbeth's operation will require the front half of the head to be shaved, so consent must be obtained.
Eyebrows are never shaved.

All pre-operative preparation to ensure the patient's safety will be carried out.

Post-operatively
The post-operative care of the patient will include:

Care of the airway with the risk of blood from the nose and naso-pharynx and possible presence of a nasal pack.
Observation of vital signs.
Nurse the patient sitting up to relieve venous congestion.
Care of any intravenous infusion or transfusion which may be in progress.
Oral fluids as soon as the patient wishes to drink.
Check urinary output.
Analgesic and antiemetic as needed.
Care of the nasal pack and removal usually in 24-48 hours.
Frequent mouthwashes, especially when there are oral sutures.
Soft diet at first, if desired.
Some assistance with hygiene may be needed.
Eye care if the eye is swollen or sore.
A face incision may be covered with a small dressing, or left exposed.
Any drainage tube removed when drainage is minimal.
Sutures removed 4-5 days to give a good cosmetic scar.

Following Caldwell-Luc operation the sinus may be washed out via the new ostia to remove any blood clot. Occasionally catheters may be left in the sinus for irrigation.

A Macbeth operation will involve considerable blood loss from the scalp incision; therefore the patient will need careful observation and monitoring. The wound will be drained at each end with tubing or vaccuum drains.

Sutures may be removed from the 7th day.

Oedema of the eye can occur and eye care must be given.

As in any other surgery where there may be intracranial involvement neurological observations may be carried out.

As with nasal surgery such things as bleeding, pain, swelling, pyrexia, eye problems, headache, should be reported.

Patient having sinus surgery will be followed up in the Out-Patient Department.

Practice Questions

1. What changes take place in the sinuses when there is an acute infection?
2. What are the possible complications of:
   a acute maxillary sinusitis
   b frontal sinusitis?
3. What is:
   a A nasal polypi
   b Antrochoanal polypi
   c Intranasal antrostomy
   d Macbeth's operation?
4. The most likely cause of acute sinusitis is:
   a A dental abscess
   b Acute rhinitis
   c Swimming and diving
   d A fractured nose?
5. Nasal polypi are most likely to be associated with:
   a Acute sinusitis
   b Acute coryza
   c Chronic frontal sinusitis
   d Allergic rhinitis?
6. With acute maxillary sinusitis any discharge will be seen in the:
   a Inferior meatus
   b Middle meatus
   c Superior meatus
   d Above the superior turbinate?
7. A Caldwell-Luc operation will be performed for:
   a Acute maxillary sinusitis
   b Chronic maxillary sinusitis
   c Chronic frontal sinusitis
   d Chronic ethmoidal sinusitis?
8. The most common form of sinusitis in children is:
   a Chronic maxillary sinusitis
   b Acute maxillary sinusitis
   c Acute ethmoidal sinusitis
   d Chronic ethmoidal sinusitis?

Mark statements 9-14 True or False

9. Frontal sinusitis is the most common form of acute sinusitis.
10. Antrum washout is never done in acute maxillary sinusitis before antibiotic treatment is given.
11. Nasal allergy may be a predisposing factor of chronic sinusitis.
12. The headache of frontal sinusitis tends to get worse towards afternoon.
13. An intranasal antrostomy is made in the middle meatus.
14. Eyebrows are never shaved prior to exploration of the frontal sinus.

15. Explain the problems and care of a patient with acute maxillary sinusitis.
16. Describe the specific post-operative care of a patient having a Caldwell-Luc operation.

Answers

1. The mucous membrane lining the sinus becomes inflamed, oedematous and produces excess mucous. Ostia becomes blocked. Ciliary action is impaired. Pus forms. Cilia is damaged. Stagnation of the secretions.
2. **a** There can be a spread of infection to other sinuses, middle ear, the throat, the chest. Also chronic sinusitis. **b** Eye involvement and intracranial infection.
3. **a** Nasal polyps are pedunculated, oedematous mucous membrane. Associated with nasal allergy or chronic infection. **b** A polypi which arises in the maxillary antrum, passes through the ostia and hangs in the post-nasal space. **c** Intranasal antrostomy is a hole made from the nose to the maxillary sinus in the inferior meatus.
   d Macbeth's operation is an operation for exploration of the frontal sinus. The scalp is reflected down to the level of the eyebrows and a bone flap raised to expose the sinuses.
4. **b**
5. **d**
6. **b**
7. **b**
8. **a**
9. False
10. True
11. True
12. False
13. False
14. True
15. The answer to the question should include:
    Patient has an acute infection, is pyrexial, feels ill, has a

headache, facial discomfort, nasal obstruction possibly a nasal discharge.
An Ear, Nose and Throat examination will be made.
Nasal swab sent for culture and sensitivity
Sinus X ray taken.

Treatment prescribed:
Systemic antibiotics — e.g. penicillin.
Steam inhalations.
Decongestant nasal drops — e.g. ephedrine.
Analgesics for pain.
Nursing care of pyrexia patient at bed rest.
Monitor temperatures and pulse 4 hourly.
Keep cool.
Encourage fluids.
Assist with hygiene and mouth care if not allowed up.
Diet as desired.
Antrum washout after a few days if symptoms do not subside.
Care and support of patient during and after this procedure.
Washout may be sent for culture and sensitivity.
Observe patient for any possible spread of infection to sinus, middle ear, throat or chest.
Patient can usually completely mobilise when acute symptoms have subsided.

16. Care of a patient after a Caldwell-Luc should include:
Care of the airway in the immediate post-operative period; there is additional risk because of blood from naso-pharynx and the presence of a nasal pack.
Nurse sitting up to relieve venous congestion when recovered from this anaesthetic.
Analgesics and antiemetics as needed.
Oral fluids commence as soon as able.
Mobilise gradually first day.
Mouth incision kept clean with mouthwashes.
Soft or ordinary diet as desired.
Change nasal bolster as needed.
Nasal pack removed usually after 24 hours rest in bed until bleeding controlled.
Ice pack may be used.
Steam inhalations and decongestant nasal drops, usually commenced a few hours after removal of pack.
All the usual post-operative care which is given to ensure patient's safety and comfort.
An antrum washout may be performed via the antrostomy to remove any blood clots.
Out-Patient follow-up.

5 THE THROAT

Structure and functions of the pharynx & larynx

The objectives of this section are to outline the structure and functions of the pharynx and larynx. Describe the more common conditions of the larynx and pharynx, the treatment and care of the patients with these conditions.

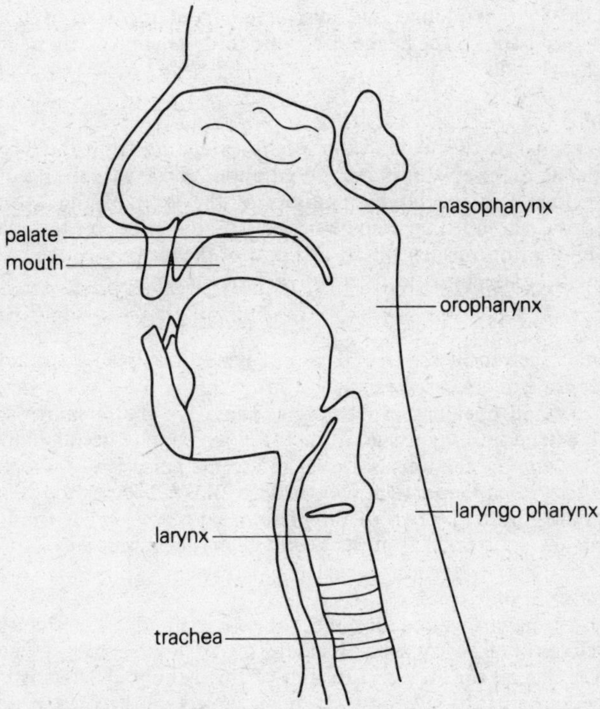

Fig 8 The pharynx

The pharynx

The pharynx is part of both the respiratory and digestive tracts. It is a muscular tube which is incomplete anteriorly except in the lower part.

Divided into three parts:

— nasopharynx
— oropharynx
— laryngopharynx or hypopharynx

Nasopharynx

The nasopharynx or post-nasal space lies behind the nasal cavity and extends from the base of the skull to the level of the soft palate. It communicates with the nose at the posterior chaenae. The Eustachian tubes protrude into the pharynx to form an elevation on the lateral walls. Situated in the midline and suspended from the roof is a mass of lymphoid tissue — the adenoids. Lymphoid tissue may also be found on the lateral walls.

Oropharynx

The oropharynx lies behind the mouth extending from the level of the soft palate to the epiglottis and is continuous above with the nasopharynx and below with the laryngopharynx at the level of the hyoid bone. Anteriorly the opening into the mouth is bordered by the uvula soft palate, anterior tonsillar pillars and part of the tongue. At the base of the tongue lies the lymphoid tissue of the lingual tonsil.

Tonsils

The palatine tonsils are two masses of lymphoid tissue surrounded by a thin capsule of connective tissue on either side of the oropharynx. On the surface small openings can be seen. These are the openings of crypts which extend into the tissue of the tonsil which may become blocked by debris. Laterally the tonsils are related to the muscles of the pharyngeal wall. They each lie between two vertical folds called the tonsillar pillars which are formed by two of the pharyngeal muscles. The tonsil can be completely enucleated from its bed of pharyngeal muscle.

Waldeyer's ring

This is the name given to the collection of lymphoid tissue which is found encircling the pharynx which includes the adenoids, the palatine tonsils and the lingual tonsil. The function of this lymphoid tissue is to aid in protection against infection. It may, however, become a focus of infection itself. Usually this lymphoid tissue atrophes at puberty.

Laryngopharynx or hypopharynx
The laryngopharynx lies behind the larynx and extends from the level of the hyoid to the cricoid cartilage. It is continuous below with the oesophagus. The anterior wall opens into the larynx at the level of the ary-epiglottic folds. Laterally the laryngopharynx extends to form two recesses called the pyriform fossae.

Muscles of the pharynx
The muscular wall of the pharynx has two layers, an external and internal layer. The external consists of three overlapping muscles, the superior, middle and inferior constrictors. The inferior has both oblique and transverse fibres, the latter forming the crico-pharyngeal sphincter at the oesophageal junction. These muscles constrict during swallowing and push the food along. In the midline, posteriorly between the oblique and transverse fibres of the inferior constrictor is a potential weakness called Killian's dehiscence which is the site where a pharyngeal pouch can occur. The internal muscles of the pharynx are concerned with shortening the pharynx, movement of the soft palate, opening the Eustachian tube on swallowing, and elevating the larynx during swallowing. Lining the pharynx is mucous membrane, of the respiratory type in the nasopharynx and stratified squamous in the remainder.

Functions of the pharynx

Digestion
The oropharynx and laryngopharynx form part of the digestive tract between the mouth and the oesophagus.

Also the pharynx is actively concerned with the mechanism of deglutition or swallowing.

Respiration
The pharynx forms the part of the upper respiratory tract between the nose, mouth and the larynx.

During swallowing the pharyngeal muscles close off the nasopharynx and nose by elevating the soft palate and so protecting them from contamination by food.

The pharynx also aids in protection of the lower respiratory tract during the act of swallowing by assisting in elevating the larynx and closing it off with the epiglottis.

Protection against infection
Waldeyer's Ring of lymphoid tissue helps protect the lower respiratory and digestive tract from infection, but may itself become the site of infection.

Speech
The pharynx helps with voice resonance and articulation.

Taste
Flavours from food pass through the pharynx to the olfactory area in the nose where they stimulate the nerve endings.

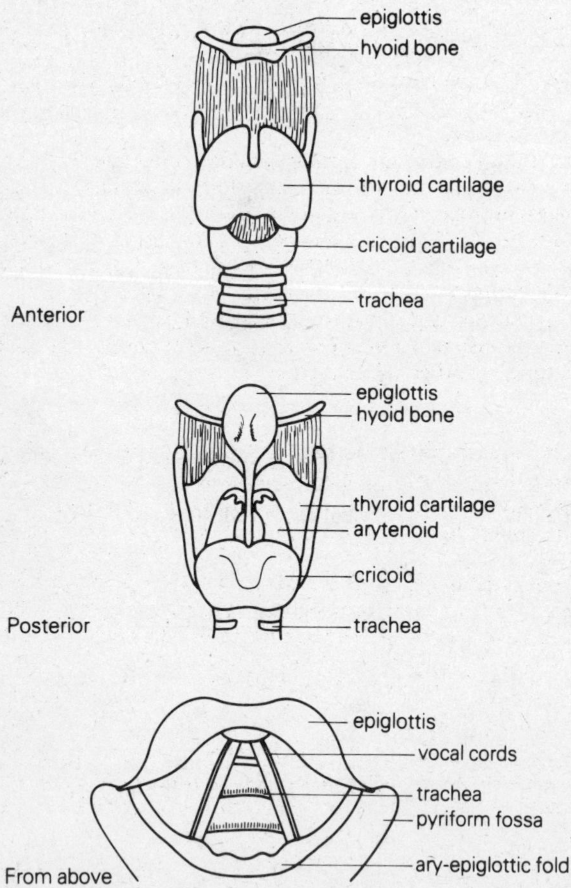

Fig 9 The larynx

The larynx

The larynx is part of the respiratory tract and also the organ responsible for voice production. It is situated in the midline of the neck in front of the pharynx at the level of the 4-6 cervical vertebrae, continuous with the oropharynx above and the trachea below.

Hyoid bone

The hyoid bone is a V shaped bone above the larynx at the base of the tongue. It gives attachment to the tongue and is linked to the larynx by means of ligaments and membranes.

The larynx is made up of a framework of cartilages.

Thyroid cartilage

This is the largest of the cartilages and is sometimes likened to an open book. Two wings or alae meet anteriorly at an angle which forms the laryngeal prominence of 'Adams Apple'. It is the difference of this angle in the male and female which accounts for the voice differences.

Cricoid cartilage

The cricoid cartilage lies below the thyroid cartilage and is shaped like a signet ring with the lamina forming the posterior part of the larynx. It is the strongest and only complete ring.

Epiglottis

This is a leaf shaped structure of yellow elastic cartilage which is situated between the tongue and the opening of the larynx, its stem attached to the upper part of the thyroid. Its function is to prevent food and foreign bodies going into the larynx.

Arytenoid cartilages

These are two pyramid shaped cartilages situated on the lamina of the cricoid cartilage. They give attachment for the vocal cords and muscles.

There are articulating joints between the cricoid and the thyroid cartilages and between the arytenoid and the cricoid. They have rotating gliding movements.

Connecting the cartilages with each other with the surrounding structures are ligaments and membranes. The upper border of one sheet of connective tissue form the ary-epiglottic fold and the lower the false vocal cord.

Vocal cords

These are two horizontal folds on each side of the larynx formed by fibrous tissue and covered by mucous membrane. They extend from the angle of the thyroid to the arytenoids. The upper folds are the false cords or ventricular folds while the lower folds which project further into the cavity are the true vocal cords. These are pearly white in colour due to their poor blood supply; they are concerned with phonation and protection of the larynx.

Between the false and true cords is a recess called the ventricle of the larynx. The area between the true cords is the glottis which is wide when the cords are abducted and a narrow slit when they are adducted.

The sub-glottic space is the area below the cords while the area above is the supraglottis.

There are two groups of muscles concerned with the larynx. One group changes the position of the larynx to adjust it for its functions. The second group is concerned with abduction, adduction and fine control of the vocal cords.

Respiratory type mucous membrane lines the larynx, except over the vocal cords where it is stratified squamous type.

Functions of the larynx

The functions of the larynx are as follows.

Respiratory

The larynx is the part of the respiratory tract between the oropharynx and the trachea.

Protection

The larynx has a protective function to prevent damage to the lower respiratory tract; this is brought about by swallowing and coughing. In swallowing when a foreign body such as food threatens to enter the respiratory tract, the larynx is drawn upwards and closed and respiration ceases.

Coughing expells secretions or foreign bodies from the respiratory tract. Air is inspired, the larynx is closed and then opened suddenly to permit forceful expulsion of air.

Phonation

This is brought about by vibrations of the vocal cords on expiration. Opening and closing of the glottis creates puffs of air which are perceived as sound.

Fixation

Fixation of the chest and abdominal muscles is aided by closure of the larynx and trapping air in the chest. This is used in musculr effort such as digging, defaecation, childbirth.

Infant larynx

The infant larynx is not only small, but relatively smaller than that of the adult and therefore the lumen is narrow.

It is more funnel shaped, the narrowest part being where it is continuous with the trachea.

The cartilages are soft and therefore can collapse and become indrawn on inspiration; therefore any swelling can readily cause respiratory difficulties and obstruction in the child and put them at risk.

Trachea

The trachea lies below the larynx and goes down into the chest where it divides into the right and left bronchus. It is made up of incomplete rings of cartilages which are completed posteriorly by muscle and connective tissue and lined by respiratory type mucous membrane. The isthmus of the thyroid gland crosses in front of the upper part of the trachea.

Practice Questions

Fill in the gaps

1. The nasopharynx extends from the level of .... to the level of ....
2. The oropharynx extends from the level of .... to the level of ....
3. The laryngopharynx extends from the level of .... to the level of ....
4. The vocal cords extend from the .... to the ....
5. The Eustachian tube connects .... and ....
6. What are:
   — Waldeyer's Ring?
   — Pyriform fossae?
   — Killian's dehiscence?
   — Tonsillar pillars?
7. What tissue lines the pharynx and larynx?
8. List the functions of the pharynx and larynx.
9. What are the functions of the:
   — Vocal cords
   — Epiglottis
   — External muscles of the pharynx
   — Laryngeal muscles?
10. Why is the infant larynx so at risk if any swelling occurs?
11. The cricoid cartilage:
    a. lies above the thyroid cartilage
    b. is the strongest cartilage

- **c.** is shaped like an open book
- **d.** is made of elastic cartilage?

12. The thyroid cartilage:
    - **a.** is the largest of the cartilages
    - **b.** is pyrimidal in shape
    - **c.** protects the laryngeal orifice
    - **d.** forms the posterior part of the larynx?
13. The arytenoid cartilages:
    - **a.** are situated on the thyroid cartilage
    - **b.** account for the difference between male and female voice
    - **c.** are shaped like a leaf
    - **d.** give attachment to the vocal cords?
14. The laryngopharynx lies:
    - **a.** in front of the larynx
    - **b.** is continuous above with the nasopharynx
    - **c.** is continuous below with the trachea
    - **d.** is continuous below with the oesophagus?
15. The glottis lies:
    - **a.** above the vocal cords
    - **b.** below the vocal cords
    - **c.** between the true cords
    - **d.** between the true and false cords?

Answers

1. the base of the skull
   the soft palate
2. the soft palate
   the hyoid bone
3. the hyoid bone
   the cricoid cartilage
4. angle of the thyroid cartilage
   arytenoid cartilages
5. the nasopharynx and middle ear
6. Waldeyer's ring — lymphatic tissue circling the pharynx includes adenoids, palatine tonsils and lingual tonsil.

   Pyriform fossae — two recesses formed where the laryngopharynx extends laterally round the larynx.

   Killian's dehiscence — a potential weakness between the oblique and transverse fibres of the inferior constrictor muscles.

   Tonsil pillars — two vertical folds between which the palatine tonsils lie, formed by two of the pharyngeal muscles.

7. Respiratory type mucosa (columna ciliated epithelium) lines the nasopharynx and the larynx, except the vocal cords.
   Stratified squamous epithelium lines the oro and laryngopharynx and the vocal cords.
8. Functions of the pharynx are:

   — being part of respiratory tract
   — being part of the digestive tract
   — concerned with swallowing
   — elevates the soft palate and prevents food contaminating the nasopharynx and nose
   — helps protect the lower respiratory tract by elevating the larynx
   — protects against infection
   — help with voice resonance and articulation
   — taste — flavours pass through the pharynx from the mouth to the nose.

   Functions of the larynx are:

   — part of the respiratory tract
   — protects the lower respiratory tract by the functions of swallowing and coughing
   — phonation
   — fixation.
9. Vocal cords:

   — protection of the larynx by closing during swallowing
   — phonation by vibration of the cords on expiration.

   Epiglottis:
   — prevents food and foreign bodies going into the larynx.

   External muscles of pharynx:

   — these are the constrictor muscles which contract and push the food along.

   Laryngeal muscles:

   — adjust the position of the larynx for its various functions
   — adduction, abduction and fine control of the cords.
10. The infant larynx is:

    — small and the lumen narrow
    — funnel shaped, the narrowest point being at the junction with the trachea
    — cartilages are soft and can easily collapse and be indrawn on inspiration.
11. **b**
12. **a**

13. **d**
14. **d**
15. **c**

Throat

The pharynx and larynx are part of the upper respiratory tract. Invariably everyone suffers from upper respiratory tract infection from time to time, symptoms related to this area are familiar to us all. Unfortunately familiarity can breed contempt and sometimes the common discomforts can be indicative of more serious disease and may go unheeded for some time.

The common symptoms which patients complain of, are sore throat, dysphagia, hoarseness, all of which may occur to varying degrees.

Sore throat

This may be caused by irritants, infection or associated with nearby infection or some general diseases.

Dysphagia

Difficulty in swallowing may be because the swallowing is painful or because of obstruction. It is a symptom which may be seen in conditions of the oropharynx, hypopharynx, oesophagus, in conditions of the chest, abdomen and with neurological problems.

Hoarseness

This may be caused by acute and chronic infection, trauma or paralysis of the vocal cords. Though a very common symptom of upper respiratory tract disease any patient with hoarseness which persists longer than about three weeks should be referred to the ENT Department.

Examination

After taking a history an examination will be made.

The oropharynx and mouth can be easily seen using a light and a tongue depressor. A warmed post nasal mirror will be used to get a view of the nasopharynx. An indirect laryngoscopy using a laryngeal mirror will be done to examine the larynx, and the upper part of the laryngopharynx. The vocal cords and their mobility can also be seen. Fibreoptic Endoscopes are now used to examine the upper respiratory tract, pharynx and oesophagus.

The neck will be palpated for the presence of any lumps.

Investigations
X ray examination — these may include:

straight X rays of the neck
X ray of chest and sinuses for associated disease
barium swallow when there is dysphagia
tomography of the neck
CAT scanning can now be used as a method of diagnosis

Endoscopy
The pharynx, larynx and oesophagus can be examined direct using the appropriate endoscope. Biopsy can be made of suspect tissue.

General investigations such as full blood profile may be done.

Swabs may be sent for bacteriology.

6 THE PHARYNX

Conditions of the pharynx

Pharyngitis
Pharyngitis, inflammation of the pharynx, may be acute or chronic.

Acute
Acute pharyngitis is something most people suffer from, from time to time usually as part of an upper respiratory tract infection such as a cold. The causal organism may be viral or bacterial, often the haemolytic streptococcus. Occasionally the inflammation can occur as a result of trauma such as swallowing hot liquids or due to a foreign body.

The patient has a red sore throat which makes swallowing difficult and may have a temperature and referred earache. Treatment is usually conservative, rest, plenty of fluids and analgesics such as aspirin. Antibiotics only if the condition is severe.

Chronic
The symptoms of chronic pharyngitis are vague, a feeling of irritation, discomfort, dryness or even a lump in the throat. There is a tendency to keep clearing the throat and the voice may become husky.

Causes may be recurrent acute attacks or secondary to infection elsewhere such as nasal, sinus or dental. It may also be irritation from smoke, alcohol or atmospheric pollution, voice strain or simple cancerphobia.

Often it is not possible to identify the cause. On examination the lymphoid tissue may be seen to be prominent.

Treatment
This is directed towards treating any co-existing infection, advice on avoiding irritants, reassurance, possible speech therapy and sometimes diathermy of the enlarged lymphoid tissue.

Tonsillitis
Infection of the tonsils is most common in children, though it does occur in adults. The causal organism is usually streptococcus. This is an acute infection so the child will be ill, is pyrexial and in fact can have febrile convulsions. The throat is sore and as it is painful to swallow the child will probably refuse food. Earache can occur from referred pain. The pharynx is red and the tonsils inflamed with the crypts filled with pus and

debris. There may be enlarged neck glands and the tongue is usually furred and unpleasant.

Treatment
This is as for any acute infection, rest, plenty of fluids, drugs such as aspirin which will be antipyrexic and analgesic, with frequent mouthwashes. Antibiotics, probably penicillin are usually prescribed after a throat swab has been taken, and the full course must be given.

Complications
The most common complication of an acute tonsillitis is a quinsy or peritonsillar abscess. However tonsillitis can pre-dispose to acute supperative otitis media, chest infection, and repeated attacks can lead to chronic tonsillitis. Other complications which can occur are acute glomerulonephritis and rheumatic fever.

Quinsy
Quinsy or peritonsillar abscess is a complication of tonsillitis. It occurs when infection spreads through the capsule into the surrounding tissues causing them to become oedematous, inflamed and for an abscess to form between the tonsil and tonsilar bed. On examination, which is difficult because of trismus, the soft palate on the affected side is swollen pushing the oedematus uvula over to the other side.

The patient is ill, pyrexial with a dry mouth, swollen neck glands and is in great discomfort. Usually the dysphagia is so severe they cannot swallow saliva and so will dribble and find it very difficult to talk properly. Referred pain will cause earache.

Treatment
This may be as for tonsillectomy with large doses of antibiotics, probably penicillin. Should an abscess have formed it can be incised using a surface anaesthetic. An incision will be made with the point of a scalpel, the blade being guarded with adhesive plaster, and the opening enlarged with an angled pair of sinus forceps. The pus will drain out giving the patient immediate relief. A mouth wash is given and a specimen of the pus sent for culture.

The patient is advised to rest, continue with frequent mouthwashes and the full course of systemic antibiotics.

Tonsils and adenoids
Tonsils and adenoids are lymphoid tissue their function is therefore to aid in protection against infection.

A child's tonsils and adenoids will begin to enlarge when they come in contact with infection which is usually when they go to playgroup, nursery or proper school. As the child acquires immunity the tissues will atrophy — the adenoids will in fact disappear altogether about puberty.

However, tonsils and adenoids can themselves become infected and also be a focus of infection. Therefore problems can be attributed to enlargement and infection.

The problems which can occur due to adenoids include:

mouth breathing and snoring

a nasal voice

the so-called 'adenoid face'

lymphoid tissue round the Eustachian tube orifice can predispose to secretory otitis

enlarged tonsils may give difficulty in swallowing and lead to loss of appetite — the child becoming a poor feeder.

Infection can lead to — tonsillitis and its complications, e.g. Quinsy — acute suppurative otitis media — sinusitis — frequent colds — nasal discharge — chest infections.

Tonsillectomy, adenoidectomy

The operation of tonsillectomy and adenoidectomy has always been one which is controversial and the problems experienced in childhood can often be self-limiting.

Indications for the operation will be at the discretion of the individual surgeon. However the most usual reasons for carrying out this operation will probably be:

recurrent tonsillitis

deafness

risk of chronic middle ear disease

loss of school time

Nursing care of a child having tonsillectomy and adenoidectomy

The operation is going to be carried out on a child so all the 'tender loving care' and psychological support for a child in hospital must be given. This will include allowing the parent to spend as much time as possible with their child.

The child is admitted the day prior to surgery. A general and an ENT examination is done. If there is a raised temperature, or any evidence of infection or recent infection the operation will almost certainly be postponed. This is because the risk of post operative bleeding is increased in the presence of infection. Note should be taken of any loose teeth or crowns as these can easily be dislodged in theatre by the gag which holds the mouth open. Bleeding and clotting times and Hb, may be done and should be within normal limits. The usual pre-operative care is given to ensure the child's safety and they should be taken to theatre by a nurse they know.

Adenoids are removed with a curette and tonsils dissected out and the bleeding points tied off.

Post operative nursing care begins as the child leaves the theatre table. The first priority is the care of the airway which can be obstructed by the tongue or the inhalation of blood or secretions. So the patient should be placed in the recovery position with the head low to enable secretions to drain from the mouth. A small child can lie with a pillow under its chest, or a tipping trolley is useful. There should always be easy access to the patient's airway in case respiratory problems occur. The jaw is supported to prevent the tongue falling back. Suction and oxygen should be at hand. However, direct suction to the tonsil bed should be avoided as this may cause bleeding. Any indication of a missing tooth should be reported at once. Loose deciduous teeth are usually removed on the table. The child's colour, pulse and respirations must be observed. When the reflexes have returned and the child can safely maintain its own airway and if there is no evidence of bleeding, the child can be taken back to the ward.

Back in the ward the child should be placed on their side supported with a pillow and carefully observed. The pulse is checked frequently probably quarter hourly, half hourly and hourly according to ward policy.

The great risk at this time is bleeding which may be indicated by:

— rise in pulse rate
— pallor
— sweating
— restlessness
— frequent swallowing
— bubbly respirations
— seeing fresh blood from the nose-mouth
— fresh blood in any vomit.

Any suspicion of bleeding must be reported immediately. A child may bleed quietly, swallow the blood, suddenly vomit and collapse.

Later the child can be washed and allowed sips of water.

The most important aspect of this post-operative care from the day after operation till discharge is that they are encouraged to eat and drink normally. If the patient does not swallow and use the pharyngeal muscles slough will form on the tonsil bed which can later separate, causing secondary haemorrhage.

Gargles are given several times a day. Often, litle children find gargling difficult though they can manage mouthwashes.

Children usually can get up the day after operation but they should stay fairly quiet. Television, books, sitting down games are indicated here and parental participation can be a great help.

Analgesics in the form of soluble aspirin, aspirin mucilage, or aspergum may be given, though some surgeons prefer aspirin *not* to be used.

Earache is sometimes complained of and is usually referred pain, however the ears should be examined to make sure they are normal.

The tonsil bed should be looked at and if there is slough formation dilute hydrogen peroxide gargles may be given.

Children are usually discharged from about the second post operative day onwards though this can vary with the child's home circumstances — such as distance from the hospital.

On discharge the mother should be advised to:

— encourage the child to eat and drink normally
— continue with the gargles
— try to prevent the child coming in contact with any infection
— who to contact should there be any problem such as bleeding
— any follow-up — the child may be seen at the Out Patient Department or the GP may indicate when school can be resumed.

Complications

Haemorrhage

Any indication of bleeding should be reported at once. Medical staff will decide if the child is to return to theatre. If bleeding is slight the patient may just be observed. This must be done with vigilance as a small child cannot afford much blood loss — they will become shocked very quickly. Usually blood is cross-matched so that it is ready should it be needed.

If a child does not have to go back to theatre it must be done quickly before his condition deteriorates. An intravenous infusion will usually be set up. Anaesthetic induction can be difficult because of the presence of blood around the airway and in the stomach. Suction must be ready at hand all the time. Bleeding vessels in the tonsil bed will be tied off. Adenoidal bleeding can be caused by a remaining tag of tissues which must be removed. A post nasal pack can be put in to stop adenoidal bleeding.

The pack is made a suitable size for the child with three strings attached. Catheters through the nose are tied to two of the strings and the pack is pulled into place. The third string will be secured to the cheek and can be used for removing the pack later.

On return to the ward a nurse will usually stay with the child to

— monitor the child's condition
— prevent the child pulling at the string of the pack if they have one
— watch the intravenous infusion/transfusion
— observe for any further bleeding
— comfort the child

Once bleeding is controlled and the blood loss replaced the child usually makes an uneventful recovery.

Secondary Haemorrhage
This can occur 5-10 days post operatively usually due to separation of slough or infection. It may be serious enough for the patient to be re-admitted when the treatment will be rest, antibiotics and appropriate treatment for blood loss.

Asphyxia
There is the risk of this in the immediate post operative period due to the presence of blood and secretions round the airway. A child's larynx can readily go into a spasm.

Lung infection
Any inhalation of blood, secretions, or a tooth could give rise to lung infection.

Acute suppurative otitis media
Ear infection can occur after tonsillectomy and adenoidectomy.

Trauma
Trauma can be caused to the lips and teeth, by the gag holding the mouth open.

Voice change
Can occasionally occur after operation.

Psychological
Any of the problems related to a child being in hospital which hopefully can be minimised by good preparation by the parents, and by allowing them to spend as much time as they wish with their child.

The care of an adult having a tonsillectomy is the same, though they may stay in hospital a little longer.

Pharyngoscopy and oesaphagoscopy
Endoscopic examination of the pharynx and oesophagus may be carried out for:

— examination and diagnostic purposes
— taking a biopsy
— removal of foreign body
— surgical procedures such as Dohlmans procedure and dilation of strictures.

After this procedure nothing should be given by mouth to the patient until ordered. It may be practice to give only fluids for some hours.

Should there be any evidence of trauma, for example with a foreign body, all food and drink may be withheld for a while. Alternatively only sterile water may be given, or fluid but not food.

Endoscopy of the pharynx and oesophagus is not without risk of perforation, so any complaint of pain in the neck or chest radiating to the back, or evidence of shock or pyrexia should be reported immediately. Perforation could cause a mediastinitis or even perforation of one of the great vessels.

Foreign bodies

Unlike foreign bodies of the nose and ear which occur mainly in children, foreign bodies which are swallowed can occur in any age group. Children eat objects such as buttons, coins, toys while adults, especially dentureless ones, tend to swallow bones, lumps of meat, bits of denture plate and get them stuck. Bizarre items like spoons and forks are sometimes swallowed by the mentally unbalanced or attention seekers!

A patient can usually give an account of being aware of what they have swallowed and are able to point to the place where they feel discomfort. Small fish bones may stick in the tonsil and can simply be removed with forceps. Other objects tend to get held up at the post cricoid region.

The patient may have severe dysphagia. Saliva can be seen pooling at the back of the throat.

A straight X ray or a barium swallow may show the foreign body, in which case the patient goes to theatre. A pharyngoscope or oesophagoscope is passed and the foreign body removed with special forceps. Should the foreign body not be seen on X ray but there is any possibility of there being one, the patient will still have an endoscope passed. Sometimes an area of trauma may be seen, caused by a passing foreign body which is still causing the discomfort.

Even if it is felt the patient does not have a foreign body, they may still be admitted for observation or allowed to go home and told to return if they are worried or the symptoms do not quickly subside.

The problem of any foreign body sticking in the pharynx or oesophagus is the risk of perforation and infection. Most patients, however, make a quick uneventful recovery after oesophagoscopy and removal of the foreign body.

Pharyngeal pouch

A pharyngeal pouch is a protrusion of mucosa which occurs at Killans dehiscence. It is seen mainly in elder men and is probably predisposed to by neuro muscular inco-ordination.

A small pouch may give no problems or only mild symptoms, but with a large pouch food will pass into the pouch on swallowing.

The patient feels the food is sticking, there is dysphagia, regurgitation or vomiting and gurgling noises from the pouch. Diagnosis is confirmed by barium swallow and oesophagoscopy.

Treatment

If the symptoms are mild probably nothing will be done. There are two methods of surgical treatment. The pouch can be removed completely using a neck incision and a myotomy done on the cricopharyngeous muscle. A naso-gastric tube will usually be passed for post-operative feeding until the tissues have healed.

An alternative form of surgery is to do a Dohlman procedure. This is often used if the patient is not fit enough for more extensive surgery. A Dohlman oesophagoscope is passed and using the relevant instruments the bridge of tissue between the pouch and the oesophagus is diathermied. The food can then pass down the oesophagus. A naso-gastric tube may be passed.

The post operative care will depend on the type of surgery, for the pouch exision, special care will be the wound care and the naso-gastric tube feeds, gradually returning to normal diet. The care after Dohlman's procedure will be as for oesophagoscopy, and maintaining the patient's nutrition.

Paterson-Brown Kelly syndrome

Paterson-Brown Kelly or Plummer Vincent syndrome is a condition most commonly seen in woman.

They usually present complaining of an increasing dysphagia, leading to weight loss. On examination they may be found to have glossitis, angular stomatitis and koilonychia. The blood profile will show an iron deficiency anaemia. Oesophagoscopy a web formation and stricture of the hypopharynx.

Appropriate treatment will be given for the anaemia.

Oesophagoscopy and dilation of the stricture will be carried out when necessary. The associated symptoms will improve.

Globus Pharyngitis

This is a condition where the patient will complain of a feeling of a lump or something in the throat. It is associated with swallowing saliva but not food — there is no weight loss. These patients tend to be anxious as they usually fear they have cancer.

Investigations will be carried out to exclude malignant disease and to find a cause. Sometimes they are found to have reflex oesophagitis which can be helped with antacids.

Once investigations show no evidence of malignant disease they can be reassured.

Practice Questions

1. What is a trismus?
   koilonychia?
   dysphagia?
2. List the clinical features of Paterson Brown Kelly Syndrome.
   How can this condition be diagnosed?
3. What is a quinsy?
   How may it be treated?
4. Conditions of the oropharynx are likely to cause
   a dysphonia
   b dysphasia
   c dysphagia
   d dyspnoea
5. What is the most likely cause of earache in a child on the first day after adeno-tonsillectomy? Is it:
   a referred pain
   b middle ear infection
   c blood in the Eustachian tube
   d too much crying
6. When caring for a child after tonsillectomy what do you observe first?
   a there is no undue bleeding
   b there are no missing teeth
   c the airway is clear
   d the operation notes are written
7. In the condition of Globus Pharyngitis the patient will complain of
   a a lump in the throat
   b difficulty in swallowing food
   c feeling tired — lethargic
   d a sore tongue
8. A female patient is admitted having swallowed a meat bone. What is the most likely place for it to have stuck?
   a pyriform fossa
   b post cricoid region

c tonsils
d cardiac sphincter

9. On return to the ward after oesophagoscopy and removal of the bone the nurse knows the patient can have
   a fluid as soon as she wishes
   b intravenous fluids only
   c sterile fluids as soon as she wishes
   d fluids when ordered
10. Following oesophagoscopy which of the following should be reported immediately?
    a chest pain radiating to the back
    b difficulty in swallowing
    c spitting up small quantities of blood
    d feeling something is still there
11. A complication of oesophagoscopy which can give most cause for concern is?
    a mucosal trauma
    b perforation
    c oesphagitis
    d oedema
12. Sarah aged 5 years is admitted for tonsillectomy and adenoidectomy. She has a brother aged 7. What care will Sarah need from the immediate post-operative period until she returns home on third post-operative day?
    What part can Sarah's mother play in her care?

Answers

1. Trismus — difficulty in opening the mouth
   Koilonychia — spoon shaped nails
   Dysphagia — difficulty in swallowing.
2. Clinical features of Paterson-Brown-Kelly syndrome:
   dysphagia, weight loss, glossitis angual stomatitis, koilynichia, tiredness, pallor.
   Blood picture will show an iron deficiency anaemia.
   Endoscopy — a web formation and stricture of hypo pharynx.
3. A quinsy is a complication of tonsillitis. There is abscess formation between the tonsil and tonsillar bed.
   Treatment — incise with a guarded scalpel and quinsy forceps. Treat for tonsillitis — antibiotics, mouthwashes, analgesics, fluids, rest.
4. **c**
5. **a**
6. **c**
7. **a**
8. **b**

9. **d**
10. **a**
11. **b**
12. Sarah's care should include:
    Recovering from anaesthetic
    Care of the airway
    Placed in the recovery position — head low
    pillow under chest
    airway *in situ*
    jaw supported
    secretions removed if necessary
    O_2 available
    check colour, respiration pulse
    check teeth
    watch for any bleeding

On return to the ward
— lie on side
— monitor pulse frequently
— observe for elevated pulse and pallor, sweating, frequent swallowing, restlessness, respirations which sound 'wet' vomiting fresh blood and seeing blood from nose or mouth
Report immediately if bleeding suspected:
— later wash, put bed clean
— give small drinks
— tender loving care.
Care until discharged:
— encourage drinking, and eating to prevent formation of slough.
— gargles or mouthwashes
— analgesics if ordered
— may get up but not be too energetic
— tonsil beds inspected
— ears looked at if any complaint of earache.
Care from Mother:
— allowed to stay, open or extended visiting
— mother can give basic care — washing, putting to bed, mouth hygiene
— should encourage Sarah 'to eat' — should understand importance of this
— can entertain Sarah
— brother should be allowed to visit.
Mother advised on care when Sarah goes home:
— importance of eating, mouth hygiene, avoid infection

— what problems may occur
— who to contact if worried
— what follow-up there will be
— when Sarah will probably be able to go back to school.

7 THE LARYNX

Conditions of the larynx

Acute laryngitis
This is acute inflammation of the larynx and is usually part of an upper respiratory tract infection. The cause may be bacterial or viral and can be pre-disposed to by conditions such as over use or abuse of the voice, smoking, alcohol or nose and sinus disease.

Clinical features
Usually the patient will have an upper respiratory tract infection, is pyrexial and feels unwell with some discomfort and tenderness of the throat and possibly a cough and slight dysphagia. The voice is hoarse, croaky and sometimes aphonic.

Indirect laryngoscopy would show the larynx to be inflammed and oedematous with a sticky mucous secretion on the vocal cords.

Treatment
This will be rest, preferably in bed with complete voice rest. Inhalations may be helpful and antibiotics may be prescribed.

Should the oedema be severe there could be a risk of airway obstruction and dyspnoea. The patient would be admitted to hospital in case tracheotomy may be necessary.

A child with its smaller, softer, larynx is more at risk from oedema and therefore could need hospital admission for observation and humidification.

Acute epiglottitis or supraglottitis
This is an acute inflammatory condition of the mucosa of the supraglottis commonsly caused by the Haemophilis influenzea B.

It occurs more often in children and is a potentially dangerous condition.

Onset is usually sudden with pain and difficulty in swallowing, so that the child will not drink and will dribble rather than swallow. The epiglottis becomes bright red and swollen which will cause a change in cry. It can also lead to inspiratory stridor and respiratory difficulties.

Treatment
A child with stridor will be admitted to hospital where it can be closely observed.

Forms of treatment may vary. One current method is to intubate the child, give the oxygen and chloramphenical, and ensure the child is hydrated.

In the adult the condition is less severe with pain and difficulty on swallowing. Treatment is antibiotic and anaglesics for the discomfort.

Laryngo — Tracheal Bronchitis

This occurs usually in children of 1-3 years of age and is an acute infection of the respiratory tract from the larynx downwards. It is usually a viral infection but can be caused by a bacteria such as haemolytic streptococcus.

The condition will probably start with an upper respiratory tract infection like a cold. Hoarseness and a croupy cough will develop. Secretions, will become tenacious, purulent and may form crusts.

Laryngeal and oedema can develop with stridor as the glottis narrows leading to dyspnoea and cyanosis. The child will be pyrexial, restless, anxious and become dehydrated. This can be a life threatening condition.

Treatment

The child should be admitted to hospital where it can be observed and emergency intubation or tracheostomy is immediately at hand if the airway is obstructed. Humidification to loosen the secretions and prevent crusting is given and plenty of fluids. If the cause is found to be bacterial, antibiotics can be prescribed. A child with a severe laryngeal infection will need close observation of the airway and a lot of nursing care. They can be anxious and frightened and will want comfort and close attention.

This will be a stressful time for the parents who will also need explanations, reassurance and support.

Chronic laryngitis

Chronic inflammatory changes may take place in the larynx and are associated with

— Upper respiratory tract infection such as nasal or sinus disease where pus is trickling down into the larynx.

— Irritation from mouth breathing again usually caused by nasal problems.

— Lower respiratory tract infection particularly chronic chest disease when pus is being coughed up through the larynx.

— Voice over-use or abuse such as shouting or not using the voice correctly.

— Irritation from dust, fumes, smoking and alcohol.

The patient may have a hoarse, tired voice with a tendency to keep clearing the throat and sometimes a dry irritating cough. There is often present, nasal, sinus and dental infection.

Indirect laryngoscopy may show the larynx looking red, sometimes oedematous or with a localised area of keratin or fibrous tissue.

A careful history may elicit employment or social factors which may be relevant. Evidence of co-existing nose and sinus infections will be looked for. Chest and sinus X-rays will be ordered. A direct laryngoscopy and biopsy of any abnormal tissue will be undertaken.

Investigations must first eliminate possible presence of malignant disease.

Treatment

Any possible causal infection must be treated.

Advice on modification of life style and voice use may be given.

Referral can be made to a speech therapist to treat and re-educate in voice use.

The larynx may undergo chronic change which may present in several ways.

Examples of these are:

Keratosis or *Leucoplakia*

This is a condition occurring mainly in men in which white patches of keratin form on the mucous membrane of the vocal cord. Treatement is by laryngoscopy and stripping of the affected mucosa and sending for histalogical examination. Unfortunately this condition tends to recurr and is a pre-malignant one. Careful follow-up is therefore necessary.

Vocal polypi

These are formed by localized oedematous mucosa of the vocal cords attached to the cords by a pedicle. The polypi bobs in and out of the glottis during respiration.

Treatment is laryngoscopy and removal of the polyp.

Vocal nodules

These are small fibous growths formed on the vocal cords where they meet and again are caused by over use and misuse.

They may be an occupational hazard in people like singers, teachers and newspaper sellers. Also possibly football and other sports fans.

Since the introduction of the procedure of microlaryngoscopy when the operating microscope, special laryngoscopes and fine instruments are used, the removal of small vocal abnormalities has now become precise. This means less cord trauma, consequently less possible vocal damage.

Multpile papilloma of the vocal cords

In this condition numerous small growths occur on the vocal cords of children mainly in the age group 5-10.

The cause is unknown but theories of viral, infection and hormonal factors are among those suggested.

These papilloma can be prevelant enough to cause airway obstruction.

A child with this condition will have a hoarse voice or even aphonia and may have stridor and dyspnoea.

If the airway is embarrased a tracheostomy must be performed and this the child can have for some time.

The usual treatment is laryngoscopy and removal of the papilloma either with forceps or by first freezing with a cryoprobe or more recently by the use of laser surgery. Other treatments such as hormone therapy have been tried.

Unfortunately the papilloma keep recurring and the child has to undergo frequent admission to hospital and operations for some time. However the papilloma do usually disappear when the child gets to puberty (but not always).

The repeated surgery will cause scarring to the cords and therefore trauma to the voice. With the increasing use of laser surgery this should improve in future.

The specific problems these children can have and may need appropraite help with are:

— possible tracheostomy for some time
— limitation of some activities such as sport and swimming
— frequent hospital admission and follow up
— poor voice
— education and peer contact can be affected
— may feel different

Special help, including educational, may have to be given to the child in addition to treatment for the condition.

Inhaled foreign bodies

Most foreign bodies which threaten to go down the airway are immediately expelled by the cough reflex. Others can be assisted by simple measures such as pressure on the abdomen from behind, slapping the back and with a child, holding it head downwards.

Small objects such as peanuts, a tooth, sweets or pins can be inhaled. They may go down into the lung or could get impacted particularly in the larynx.

Removal will be by endoscopy. In some circumstances an emergency tracheostomy could be needed.

Laryngoscopy

Laryngoscopy is usually for

— diagnostic purposes
— removal of new growths e.g. vocal nodes
— to biopsy suspect tissue
— surgical procedures such as cyro and laser surgery

Care of the patient
The airway must be watched carefully in the post operative period because the instrumentation could cause swelling which would lead to repiratory obstruction. Also any blood trickling down can provoke laryngeal spasm.

Nothing should be given by mouth until ordered because the larynx may have been sprayed with a local anaesthetic, so this must have worn off and the cough and swallow reflexes returned before drink is given.

Laser surgery
Laser is now being increasingly used in some aspects of E.N.T. work such as in the mouth and larynx.

A laser is a highly precise instrument, is used with the operating microscope and no other instrumentation is needed except for suction.

With application of the laser beam, tissue is immediately destroyed, nerve endings blood and lymph vessels sealed.

This means there is minimal or no bleeding, no post-operative slough and oedema or airway problems and less risk of infection spread.

The patient experiences little or no post-operative pain and even when the mouth is involved is able to eat normally after operation.

Healing is very rapid so the patient recovers and can be out of hospital quickly.

Laser surgery can be used for such lesions, as small nodules, polyps, papilloma or ulcers. In some circumstances it can be used for pre-malignant and malignant conditions.

Practice Questions

1. What is a possible complication of
   a Laryngoscopy
   b Laryngeal Keratosis
   c Acute epiglottitis (supra-glottis)?
2. What is a
   a Vocal nodule?
   b Vocal polypi?
3. List pre-disposing causes of chronic laryngitis.
4. What is stridor?
5. What are the advantages to a patient having a lesion in the mouth removed by laser?

Answers

1. **a** Airway obstruction
   b It is a pre-malignant condition
   c Airway obstruction
2. Fibrous growth formed on the vocal cord where they meet. Localized oedematous mucosa of the vocal cord.
3. Upper respiratory tract infection.
   Lower respiratory tract infection.
   Voice use and abuse.
   Irritation e.g. dust.
4. A harsh crowsing sound caused by respiratory obstruction.
5. Advantages to patient:
   — no bleeding
   — little or no pain
   — no oedema or airway problems
   — no slough
   — can eat normally
   — rapid healing
   — short stay in hospital.

8 MALIGNANT DISEASES OF THE EAR NOSE AND THROAT

The objectives of this section are to:

1. Describe briefly how malignant disease may present in the head and neck.
2. Identify the problems of patients suffering from these diseases.
3. Explain the relevant care of patients undergoing treatment for some of these malignancies.

Malignant disease in ENT

Patients may be seen in the ENT Department presenting with malignant tumours of the ear, nose, sinuses, mouth, pharynx and larynx.

The most common site being the larynx.

Patient's problems can include:

dysphagia
dysphonia
dyspnoea
pain
deafness
nasal obstruction and discharge
eye problems
ulceration
lumps in the neck.

Investigations will be carried out and the appropriate treatment decided upon. This may be surgery, radiotherapy, chemotherapy or combined therapy.

Special problems which may arise from surgery are:

Mutilation and alteration of body image.
A tracheostomy either permanent or temporary may have to be performed.
Loss of speech resulting in breakdown in communication.
Difficulty with eating and possibly tube feeding for some time.
Reconstruction using grafts may have to be undertaken.

Pre-operative care

This may include:

Improving the patient's nutritional state.
Correcting any dehydration, anaemia, electrolyte imbalance.
Checking the bowel function-urine analysis.
Investigation such as blood profile and cross-match.

Chest X-ray.
E.C.G.
Any necessary dental treatment.
Physiotherapy.
Involving any other members of the hospital team for special care.
Giving explanation, support, reassurance to patients and relatives.
Preparation of the operation site and other areas involved.

Post-operatively

Post-operative care will be planned to meet the patient's needs, such as:

Caring for the airway including tracheostomy care.

Observing and monitoring the patient's condition.

Maintaining hydration and nutrition which may be care of intravenous infusions, tube feeding either continually or intermittently, or oral diet.

Providing relief from pain and discomfort.

Giving appropriate care to wounds and wound drainage.

Ensuring personal hygiene and skin care.

Maintaining oral hygiene.

Help with any problems of elimination such as those related to forms of feeding.

Helping with mobility.

Reinforcing and encouraging care given by others e.g. physiotherapists, speech therapists.

Maintaining good communications.

Ensuring all medication is given.

Providing a positive and practical attitude towards rehabilitation.

Giving good psychological support to patient and relatives particularly when surgery has caused an alteration in body image.

Tracheostomy

The ENT ward is probably the place in the hospital where there are most patients who have tracheostomies.

Student and pupil nurses are often rather anxious about caring for these patients but they should always remember that a patient with tracheostomy is safer than one with an obstructing airway.

Tracheostomy may be performed for many reasons but those in ENT are usually performed for some form of respiratory obstruction.

These may be

Congenital — e.g. laryngeal web

Trauma — e.g. cut throat wounds, inhalation of steam, accident trauma

Infection — e.g. acute laryngotracheal bronchitis

Tumours — benign, e.g. multiple papilloma
— malignant of tongue, pharynx, larynx

They may be performed for patients with malignancies:
- — in advanced disease
- — as part of major head and neck surgery
- — where radiotherapy causes, or may cause, swelling.

Bi-lateral nerve palsy — these can occur where there is damage to the recurrent laryngeal nerves such as after thyroidectomy.

Tracheostomies performed for other medical surgical reasons may be nursed in the ENT unit.

A tracheostomy may be temporary or permanent. Temporary such as when there is an inflammatory reaction or when it is anticipated swelling could occur, for example with lower jaw surgery.

Permanent tracheostomies may be for malignant disease, vocal cord paralysis and always as part of laryngectomy.

Tracheostomy may be an emergency procedure or elective.

An emergency tracheostomy is carried out where there is airway obstruction due to swelling or the presence of something such as a tumour blocking the airway.

The elective procedure is usually part of major surgery or in anticipation of an emergency situation arising.

Pre-operative preparation

In the emergency situation this will be reduced to the explanation and reassurance time allows.

Otherwise the pre-operative preparation will be a neck shave for a man, explanation, reassurance and support from the staff.

The operation may be carried out under general or local anaesthetic.

An incision is made, the tissue dissected and the thyroid isthmus usually divided and sutured. A hole is cut in the 3rd and 4th tracheal ring — a suture may be put from the trachea to the skin. Alternatively a small flap may be cut reflected forwards and sutured to the skin. This is a Bjork flap.

In performing the tracheostomy the surgeon has overcome the problem of obstruction but has created other problems for the patient.

These will be the interruption of the normal airway in place of which is a tube which can get blocked or displaced. The new airway has bi-passed the beneficial effect of the nose and pharynx — also the cough reflex is not so effective. Only by closing the lumen of the tube can the patient speak.

The patient will therefore need help with humidification of the inspired air, removal of secretions, care of the tube and help with communication.

Equipment put ready for the care of the patient must include:

— a working suction machine, sterile gloves and catheters
— some form of humidifier or nebulizer with an oxygen or air supply
— a spare sterile tracheostomy tube the same size and type as the patient has in
— tracheal dilators
— the patient's call system

Other equipment such as dressing, tissues, writing materials or picture cards are put out as ward practice.

The patient's needs will be assessed and the nursing care planned to meet these needs.

Nursing care

The patient will return from theatre usually with a cuffed tube in and will be nursed sitting up.

Instructions regarding the tube will be carried out.

Humidification is given via a tracheostomy mask to help prevent crusting of secretions.

Tracheostomy suction will be carried out as needed as the cough reflex is not so effective.

Procedure will vary according to local practice but common principles are:

— this is an aseptic technique using sterile catheters and gloves
— suction is only applied on withdrawal of the catheter
— catheters are used only once

The catheter should be no bigger than half the lumen of the tube. This is to ensure that there is space for air to go into the airway to take the place of air being sucked out, otherwise atelectasis can occur.

Suction can be very distressing for the patient so must be carried out carefully.

Care of the stoma is important because the surrounding skin can quickly become sore from secretions being coughed up.

Keyhole type dressings are generally used. The skin should be kept clean and dry, barrier creams may be used or products like stomadhesive can be put under the tube to protect the stoma.

Tracheostomy tubes

There are a variety of tracheostomy tubes and an appropriate one will be selected for the patient.

Tubes may be cuffed or non-cuffed.

Cuffed tubes

The inflatable cuff forms an air-tight fitting.

They will be used

— during operations
— when there is risk of blood or secretions trickling down the airway
— when a patient is being ventilated

Cuffed tubes may be deflated according to the surgeon's wishes. An inflated cuff can cause tracheal damage. With the introduction of low pressure cuffed tubes the cuff can now be safely inflated for longer periods of time.

Non-cuffed tubes

These may be metal or synthetic materials and both are expensive. Although the synthetic may look like plastic they are not usually disposable. A tracheostomy set is made up of an outer tube, an inner tube and an introducer with an obturator end which facilitates the insertion of the outer tube. The inner tube is always made slightly longer than the outer tube so that if secretions block the end of the tube the inner tube can easily be removed and the outer tube remains patent. A 'Negus' set has a second inner tube with a speaking valve so that the patient can talk without using their finger to block the lumen of the tube.

Changing a tracheostomy tube

This again will be carried out according to local practice. Inner tubes can be removed, cleaned, sterilized and replaced frequently.

Outer tubes are usually left 3–4 days post-operatively to allow the tract to become established. They can then be changed as necessary.

When changing the outer tube tracheal dilators should always be available in case of difficulties in introducing the new tube.

The procedure is first explained to the patient. Using the introducer, the new tube which may be lubricated, with for example sterile glycerine, is put into place immediately the dirty tube is removed. This causes the patient to cough so the tube is steadied in place until this ceases and the tapes can be tied. Tubes are usually tied with double tapes either side of the neck with a reef knot. This may vary with local practice. After changing a tube it should be checked that the airway is clear and the patient breathing comfortably. Care should always be taken not to damage tubes when cleaning and sterilizing. A rough edge can traumatise the trachea.

Tracheostomy sets must be kept intact as the pieces are not interchangable and new sets are expensive.

Complications

These may include the following.

Haemorrhage
This could be post-operatively, from erosion by growth or damage from the tube.

Surgical Emphysema
Emphysema of the neck can occur in the immediate post-operative period. Usually the skin sutures are removed and the air is absorbed.

Apnoea
This possibly could happen when a patient has been obstructing slowly and has a high PCO_2 which is stimulating the respiratory centre. Once the patient is tracheostomised the PO_2 will go up and the respiratory centre will lose the stimulus it has been used to.

Lung collapse
Could be caused by:
— too large a suction catheter
— low tracheostomy causing the tube to go into a bronchus
— blockage by a plug of mucous if humidification has not been adequate.

Obstruction
Due to blockage or displacement of the tube.

Crusting
Drying of secretions can cause crusting. Sometimes the instillation of a small amount of normal saline may be ordered with suction.

Skin excoriation
This will be due to the coughing of secretions onto the skin. Patients receiving radiotherapy treatment are most at risk.

Mucosal Ulceration
Can occur from trauma from the tube or poor suction technique.

Infection
From coughing up infected secretions or introduced from outside.

Psychological
This operation alters body image, the patient may feel abnormal and dirty and may isolate themseves from other people. They may be anxious about managing the tube at home.

Also the realization that their airway is more at risk than normally.

Here the encouragement and support of the nurse can be of great value.

Rehabilitation

The patient must be taught how to manage the tube and be capable of doing so before going home. It is helpful if a relative can also be taught.

On discharge they should have a supply of equipment, know how to get replacements and who to contact should they have problems.

Advice can be given on suitable clothing at the neck. Men may wear a loose collar and tie, cravat, or neck 'protector'. Women, a fine scarf, necklace or crochet 'bib'. It is desirable to avoid dusty smoky atmospheres or infection if possible. They must of course be careful not to let water go down the stoma.

A patient with a temporary tracheostomy will usually be decanulated before they go home.

The way this is done may vary

— a smaller sized tube may be used
— the tube half covered
— then completely covered

When the patient and staff are happy the patient can breath normally the tube is removed and the stoma closes and heals rapidly.

Malignant disease of the larynx

Malignant tumours of the larynx are seen more often in males than females and are usually squamous cell carcinomas. Predisposing factors are smoking and sometimes chronic voice strain. The outcome of the condition will depend very much on its site and how soon it is treated.

Sites of occurrence

The growth may be glottic, that is they arise on the vocal chords and may remain confined for some time because the cords have a poor blood supply and little lymphatic drainage. Hoarseness occurs early and providing the patient is referred to an ENT Department and treated, prognosis is very good.

Supra-sub glottic growths are above and below the cords respectively. There is more room for enlargement before symptoms develop and metastases can spread via the venous and lymphatic drainage.

Clinical features

Hoarseness is the most important symptom and any patient with hoarseness for more than about three weeks should be referred.

Other symptoms may be

— a feeling of vague discomfort
— cough
— dysphagia with pharyngeal involvement

— stridor and dyspnoea
— referred earache
— enlarged neck glands
— sometimes the patient may present with a lump in the neck indicating that by this time the tumour has already metastasised.

Diagnosis
The clinical diagnosis is confirmed by laryngoscopy and biopsy of what may be anything from a small nodule to a large fulminating mass. Vocal cords may be fixed or mobile.
Neck tomography and CAT scan can help assess the extent of the disease.

Treatment
The most appropriate treatment for each patient is decided. This may be surgery or radiotherapy. Radiotherapy is usually the choice for small tumours or as palliative treatment if the tumour is very large and inoperable.
Surgery may be used as the primary treatment if the tumour has begun to spread or with recurrence if the radiotherapy has not been completely successful.
They may be used as combined therapy and sometimes cytotoxic drugs may be given.

Laryngectomy
Laryngectomy is the removal of the larynx and is often combined with a block dissection of the neck glands on one side.

Pre-operative preparation
The patient will probably be admitted a few days prior to surgery to prepare them physically and psychologically. This preparation requires a team effort and includes the medical and nursing staff, physiotherapist, speech therapist, sometimes the medical social worker and a patient who has undergone a laryngectomy.
The medical staff will
— carry out routine examinations
— order pre-operative investigations
— explain again about surgery — that there will be a permanent tracheostomy and a loss of voice but they will be taught a different way of speaking.
Nursing staff will carry out the pre-operative care which can include providing extra nutrition if the patient has lost weight, checking the patient is not constipated. Preparing the skin area, shaving chin to mid

chest and the neck to the tip of the mastoid process on the side of the block dissection. Provide support and reassurance to the patient and family.

A physiotherapist will visit, explain about post operative care and possibly start chest treatment. Will reinforce advice on not smoking if the patient is still doing so.

The speech therapist has an important part to play in the patient's rehabilitation.

Pre-operatively their role is to assess the kind of person the patient is — if they are well motivated; what their voice is like; their background and if they have a supportive family. A speech therapist must give the patient confidence that they will speak again.

There may be problems for the medical social worker to deal with especially if the patient is not going to be able to return to their normal work.

A person who has had a laryngectomy is usually willing to visit the patient. Their appearance and ability to talk can be a great morale booster.

Operation

A block dissection of the glands on one side of the neck is performed if they are involved and the larynx is removed. The cut end of the trachea is brought forward and sutured to the skin of the neck forming the tracheal stoma. The exposed pharynx is then carefully repaired in layers.

Two or three vacuum drains will be placed under the skin flaps.

The neck wound when sutured may be left exposed, be sprayed with a dressing spray or covered with light dressing.

A cuffed tracheostomy tube will be left.

Generally a naso-gastric tube will be passed before the pharynx is closed, for post-operative feeding. Some surgeons, however, prefer to use intravenous infusion for a few days and then start oral fluids.

The problems which the patient now has will be:

- discontinuity of the normal airway
- a permanent tracheostomy
- a vulnerable airway
- disturbance of the pharynx involving swallowing
- sutured repair of the pharynx which could be at risk from breakdown
- loss of voice
- inability to communicate normally
- less able to strain.

Post operative care

The patient will be nursed in a high priority area and will probably have one nurse staying with them on return from theatre. They will be nursed sitting up with the head well supported and the neck slightly flexed.

In the immediate post operative period the care will be for any patient having major neck surgery.

This will be

— observation of vital signs
— care of the intravenous infusion or transfusion
— care of the tracheostomy
— continuous humidification
— suction as needed
— any care of the cuff that is ordered
— observation of the wound
— care of the vacuum drainage
— give analgesics to prevent pain — these should not be drugs which depress respiration
— prevention of vomiting or putting strain on the pharyngeal sutures by giving anti-emetics, also the naso-gastric tube can be aspirated if the patient is nauseated.
— check urinary output
— record fluid balance
— give mouthwash and skin care
— ensure the call bell is at hand
— talk to the patient in a normal way and have writing materials at hand

The patient's continuing nursing care will be accordng to ward practice after assessing the patient's individual needs.

This will include:

Care of the tracheostomy

— Continuous humidification which will be gradually discontinued as the patient's respiratory mucosa adapts to the changed airway
— Suction as needed until the patient is able to cough up secretions unaided.
— The cuffed tube is usually replaced by a laryngectomy tube after 2–3 days. A laryngectomy tube is shorter and broader with a slightly different curve to the tracheostomy tube. The inner tube can be changed frequently and the outer tube changed as ordered or as necessary.
— A laryngectomy tube may be left out after the stoma is healed and the sutures removed. The stoma cannot close but a tracheal 'button' can be worn as desired.

Monitoring of patient's condition
Recording of patient's temperature, pulse, blood pressure.

Chest physiotherapy
Patients must be encouraged to continue with their chest physiotherapy.

Maintain hydration and nutrition
The intravenous infusion will be discontinued when the patient is getting adequate tube feeds and the electrolytes are in balance.

Tube feeds will be commenced the day after operation with water, gradually building up to half strength and then full strength feeds ensuring the patient does not become nauseated and vomit.

Feeds may be given continuously or intermittently. All tube feeds should be given carefully to prevent the discomforts caused by tube feeding.

At some point when the surgeon decides, the patient will be given a test drink of coloured fluid such as blackcurrent juice. The neck is closely watched and providing there is no leakage oral fluids can be commenced proceeding to soft food and then normal diet.

Ensuring elimination
Fluid balance is monitored. The patient will be given appropriate treatment for any constipation or diarrhoea caused by the feeds.

Wound care
The neck wound is observed and dressed if this is the practice.

Vacuum drains are removed when drainage is minimal.

Neck sutures will be ready for removal about 7–10 days and tracked sutures about 10 days. Healing can be delayed if the neck has been irradiated.

The tracheal stoma must be kept clean and a keyhole dressing is worn for a while.

Maintaining hygiene and skin care
Pressure-area care is given. Help will be given with personal and oral hygiene. Patients are usually self-caring fairly quickly.

Encouraging mobility
The patient can get out of bed the day after operation, mobility is usually restricted by the equipment needed for the patient's care.

Giving of prescribed drugs
These will include analgesics, anti-emetics and antibiotics which will normally be given prophylactically.

Maintaining communication
Patients should be talked to in the normal way.

Writing materials should be available and picture cards can also be useful.

Complications which can occur after laryngectomy may be:

Haemorrhage
This must be observed for in the immediate post-operative period as after any major surgery.

Respiratory
Respiratory problems could be crusting of secretions, blockage of the tube or chest infection.

Wound
Infection and breakdown could occur. Poor healing is a risk when there has been radiotherapy treatment given.

Pharyngeal fistula
A fistula can develop where the pharynx has been repaired. Again, more likely if the tissues have been irradiated. Healing can take some time with the patient being tube fed and their stay in hospital prolonged.

Electrolyte imbalance
The patients electrolyte balance can be upset post-operatively. Occasionaly removal of the parathyroids can cause a calcium deficiency. Replacement therapy is given.

Stenosis
A laryngectomy stoma may gradually stenose over a period of time. Wearing a tube or button at night can help prevent this.

Rehabilitation
The post-operative care of the patient is directed towards getting the patient back to home, family and normal life.

Laryngectomy is a mutilating operation, one which alters body image as the patient now has a permanent tracheostomy and has to acquire a new way of communication. Here the nurse can do much to advise, help, support and give confidence.

The patient must know how to look after their stoma and be given the choice of a tube or button to wear either all the time, at night, or not at all. They should be advised to avoid if possible, situations such as dusty, smoky atmospheres, respiratory infections and, of course, be careful about water. Advice on clothes for the neck can be given and they should know who to contact if they have problems.

Speech therapy will be continued after discharge though distance and travel can be a problem. Some people get better oesophageal voices than others. A few never get the knack. There are artificial means of forming speech such as a mechanical vibrator or an artificial larynx.

A technique is now being developed to make a fistula in the posterior tracheal wall which is closed by a one way valve. Air can pass through this to the pharynx and be used to form speech.

Most patients who are still working should be able to return to their employment. Some jobs however may not be suitable, such as heavy manual work, work which can put a demand on the voice or where the atmosphere is unsuitable. Different employment or possible early retirement may have to be considered.

However, patients should be able to lead a full social life. There are laryngectomy clubs in some areas. Here patients who have had laryngectomies and their relatives can meet to talk over problems and socialize.

After laryngectomy most patients make a very good recovery and return to a full and active life.

Malignant disease of pharynx

The majority of pharyngeal malignant tumours are squamous cell carcinomas. However the features of the disease will vary according to its site.

Naso-pharynx

Malignancies of the naso-pharynx are fortunately rare in this country but are common in the Far East particularly in the Chinese race.

The tumour originates in the roof or wall of the naso-pharynx and quickly spreads to surrounding structures.

Clinical features depend on which direction the tumour invades. Therefore patients may present with various symptoms which means the primary growth is not always easily recognisable.

Many patients may already have a neck lump when they are first seen, indicating that it has already spread to the lymphatics. Other patients are seen in the ENT Department with unilateral deafness caused by secretory otitis media because of Eustachian tube blockage.

Nasal obstruction or epistaxis may bring them, or pain and numbness over the trigeminal nerve distribution.

Again they may be seen in the Eye Department with diplopia or squint because the cranial nerves controlling the eye muscles are affected. Other cranial nerves which may be involved are the ix x xi causing sensory and motor loss to the pharynx and larynx.

Diagnosis will be made by biopsying the post nasal space. X-rays will show erosion of the bone.

The position at the base of the skull makes the prognosis of this condition poor.

Radiotherapy and possibly cytotoxic chemotherapy will be given. Neck glands may be removed.

Hypo-pharynx

Tumours of the hypo-pharynx usually occur either in the post-cricoid region which is the lowest part of the hypo-pharynx or the pyriform fossae. Post-cricoid carcinomas are more common in women and those of the pyriform fossae in man.

Dysphagia with associated weight loss is usually the presenting symptoms of patients with a post-cricoid tumour. While the patient with a pyriform fossae lesion may complain of discomfort in the throat, dysphonia, and have enlarged nodes in the neck.

Investigations such as barium swallow, endoscopy and biopsy will help confirm the clinical diagnosis.

Treatment will be surgery or radiotherapy. Although the first choice is surgery it may not be appropriate because the disease has spread — so radiotherapy treatment will be given.

For a pyriform fossa carcinoma often a laryngectomy and partial pharyngectomy can be performed and the pharynx closed. A block dissection will be done if the glands are involved.

Surgery for post-cricoid carcinoma is laryngo-pharyngectomy, that is removal of the larynx and pharynx, and again, usually the glands on one side.

A permanent tracheostomy is given as in laryngectomy.

The pharynx is replaced by reconstructing a new food passage either by:

— viscus transposition — bringing up a piece of large bowel or the stomach from the abdomen through the chest or a tunnel made under the skin

— viscus transplantation by microvascular anastamosis of bowel segment

— using a tubed flap

— prosthetic tube

As a result of the dysphagia the patient can be very under-nourished. Means must be instigated to feed them either parentaly, by naso-gastric tube or a gastrostomy may be performed.

Laryngo pharyngectomy with Colon Transplant

This is very major surgery for any patient to undergo. The suitability for a patient for this operation must be assessed by a general surgeon as well as the ENT surgeon. They will work together as this is a combined procedure.

Pre-operative preparation

This will be as for a laryngectomy plus the preparation of the abdomen and bowel as the general surgeon wishes.

The bowel must be very clean before operation; this can be achieved by using whatever methods are current practice.

Suitable bowel sterilizing drugs will be prescribed.

Fluids only will be given the day prior to operation.

The shave will extend from the chin and mastoid process — if neck glands are to be dissected, to the knees.

Prophylactic antibiotics will be commenced. A urinary catheter is passed prior to going to theatre.

During this time the patient and relatives will need a great deal of support and reassurance.

The larynx and pharynx are removed and probably neck glands on one side.

A laparotomy is performed and a piece of colon with a good blood supply is selected and resected with the mesentery. The divided ends of the bowel are anastamosed. One end of the colon graft is anastomosed to the stomach the other end is taken through a prepared tunnel on the chest wall. The end of the sternum and a piece of clavical are removed to accommodate it. It can also be taken through the chest. In the neck the end of the colon is anastomosed to the oropharynx and the wound closed with vacuum drainage. The closure of the abdominal wound may or may not be with drainage.

A feeding tube can be passsed down the colon or a gastrostomy may have been performed for feeding purposes.

Post-operative care

The patient has undergone very major surgery and therefore will need careful observation and may be nursed in the intensive care unit for 24-72 hours.

Care of the patient's neck and tracheostomy will be as for a laryngectomy.

The abdominal care will be as the general surgeon directs.

The naso-gastric tube will be aspirated and tube feeds gradually introduced when bowel sounds are present. A test drink will be given some time after the tenth day and oral fluids commenced if there is no leak.

The urinary catheter will be left in for several days.

Drains will be removed when drainage is minimal.

Abdominal sutures can be removed from about 10th day when the wound has healed.

Speech therapy can be started when tissues are healed and the patient is fit enough.

All the nursing care and psychological support needed by a patient who has undergone major surgery will be given.

Rehabilitation is the same as for laryngectomy though the patient is generally advised to eat smaller meals.

Complications

These may be any that can arise with laryngectomy or after abdominal surgery. Necrosis of the colon is a serious complication which can occur. If the blood supply to the colon is not adequate it will necrose and have to be removed. This can greatly reduce the patient's chance of recovery.

When the post-operative period goes well the patient can be eating normally and out of hospital in about three weeks.

Laryngo pharyngectomy and reconstruction using a tubed flap

The defect left after the pharynx is removed may be reconstructed using a tubed flap. There are various techniques for this — some which may be staged. Although the time in hospital is expected to be longer than for a colon transposition morbidity and mortality rates are less.

Pre-operatively preparation will be as for a laryngectomy but with additional shaving of the abdomen and thighs as these are the skin donor areas.

The laryngo pharyngectomy and, if necessary, removal of neck glands is carried out. Different techniques may be used for reconstruction.

A flap is raised, tubed and then anastomosed to the oropharynx and the oesophagus. It may either be covered temporarily with a skin graft and the pedicle divided after several weeks (deltopectoral flap) or may lie subcutaneously in a one stage procedure (myoculaneous flap).

Split skin is used to cover the doner area from where the flap has been raised. This may not be done until the first day so there is less risk of bleeding under the new skin.

A dressing such as proflavine wool can be put over the area.

The split skin donor areas are dressed with tulle gras or similar dressing and a non-stick gauze such as meloline is put on top and secured in place with bandage and tape.

A feeding tube is passed unless a previous gastrostomy has been done. The tracheostomy tube will have the flanges cut off and may be secured with a stitch. This is to prevent any pressure on the flap.

Post-operative care will be as for a laryngectomy but with the additional care of the grafts.

Bowel sounds should be checked before tube feeding is commenced.

There must be no tension or pressure on the graft so the head is positioned towards the tube and the tracheostomy tube has no flanges.

The graft should be watched carefully and should be warm, pink and have a good venous return. Any indication of it becoming cold, blue, mottled oedematous or inflamed should be reported immediately.

The donor area is left undisturbed for 7–10 days and then the dressing is removed. If the site is healed a light protective dressing is applied and any unhealed areas can be cleaned and redressed. When the dressing is finally removed cream can be applied to get the area supple.

The skin donor area is not touched — only repacked if oozing. After about 7-10 days the dressing can be soaked off in the bath.

In some reconstructions a small fistula can leak saliva onto the chest. The skin must be clean and dry.

With some procedures the patient has to return to theatre after a few weeks for further surgery to the reconstructed area.

Oral feeding can be commenced when the tissues are healed.

Rehabilitation will be as for a laryngectomy.

The operation involves a lengthy hospitalization, therefore the patient will need a lot of encouragement and psychological support.

Oropharynx

Tumours of the oropharynx tend to occur in the tonsillar region. They may present as an ulcer of the tonsil or pharyngeal wall or one tonsil may be enlarged.

The patient may complain of dysphagia, referred earache or bleeding from the ulcerated area. A lump in the neck will indicate spread.

Treatment

Radiotherapy is usually the first choice of treatment.

Surgery may also be undertaken. This may vary for excision of the affected area and some surrounding tissue to extensive surgery.

Repair may be by primary suturing, skin graft or a forehead flap. A temporary tracheostomy may be performed as there is a risk of post-operative swelling which could cause respiratory obstruction.

Care of patient after commando or composite operation
This type of surgery may be performed for malignant disease of the oral cavity, oral pharynx and tongue.

It will include excision of the tumour and surrounding tissue which may involve removing part of the pharyngeal wall, tongue, floor of the mouth, mandible and dissection of neck glands. Repair may be achieved by primary closure, lining the cavity with split skin graft or raising a forehead flap and passing it through an incision into the mouth.

A temporary tracheostomy may be performed because of the risk of oedema and a naso-gastric tube passed for post-operative feeding.

Pre-operative preparation
As for any major head and neck surgery with possible skin graft repair.

Post-operative
Again, as for extensive surgery, the special area of care being:

— the tracheostomy which later will be allowed to close
— maintain the patient's hydration and nutrition
— naso-gastric tube feeding until the area is healed and the progression from fluid to normal diet.
— oral care using mouth washes or gentle swabbing with a gloved finger or gentle irrigation
— care of wound and wound drainage
—care of any grafts and donor area
— helping the patient with any special difficulties
— reassurance about facial appearance

The nose

Malignant tumours of the nose are uncommon. They may arise on the lateral wall, the septum or the ethmoids.

First symptoms are most likely to be nasal obstruction and epistaxis. With the close proximity of the eye and the brain, eye symptoms and CSF rhinorrhea can occur.

Treatment is usually radiotherapy. Surgery may be performed and defects can be reconstructed using grafts. Good cosmetic results can be achieved with prosthesis.

Maxilla

Tumours arising in the Maxillary sinus have usually spread by the time symptoms appear. From the sinus the tumour can destroy the surrounding bone and can spread into the tissues in any direction. The nose cheek palate and orbit can become invaded and symptoms will depend on what structures are involved.

Nasal obstruction and a blood stained discharge are usually the first symptoms experienced.

Other clinical features may be:

- — diplopia, and proptosis with orbital invasion
- — swelling, ulceration of the palate
- — teeth may become loose
- — epiphora if the naso-lacrimal duct is involved
- — swelling and ulceration of the cheek
- — pain in the face, ear, mandible
- — numbness of part of the face
- — lymphatic spread later

Diagnosis can be confirmed by X-rays showing bone destruction and a biopsy can be taken either from the nose or using a Caldwell Luc Approach.

Treatment is generally by combined radiotherapy and surgery.

Surgery will be either a partial or total maxcillectomy which sometimes may be extended if the disease has spread and can include removal of the eye.

With a partial maxcillectomy the palate is divided down the mid-line and removed with the alveoli on the affected side.

The tumour mass is removed and the cavity packed with ribbon gauze impregnated with, for example Whiteheads varnish, and held in place by a dental plate.

A permanent dental plate with an obturator to fill the defect is fitted when the pack is removed.

The cavity can be inspected and any visible recurrent tumour treated with diathermy or cryoprobe or laser.

When the whole of the maxilla is removed an external incision is made from near the corner of the eye down the side of the nose to the collumella and then splitting the upper lip in the mid-line. After removal of the maxilla, a pack again probably of Whiteheads varnish will be put into the cavity supported by a dental plate and left for about three weeks. When it is removed usually in theatre a special dental plate will have been made which will support the soft tissues.

When the eye has become infiltrated the operation will be extended to remove the orbital contents. The orbit can then be grafted with a forehead flap and a good cosmetic result obtained with a prosthesis.

Nursing care

The care of the patient pre- and post-operatively will be as for all extensive ENT surgery.

Special areas of care

Maintaining good oral hygiene with frequent mouthwashes or gentle swabbing using a gauze wrapped gloved finger instead of forceps.

Encouraging the patient to take adequate fluids and offering suitable food.

Care of the face incision and removing sutures early when healed to give a good scar.

Giving eye care and treatment when necessary.

Care of any skin grafts.

Reassurance about the cosmetic outcome of the operation.

The ear

The pinna may be the site of a carcinoma or a rodent ulcer. Treatment will be irradiation or surgery. A prosthesis can give a good cosmetic result after excision of the pinna.

A tumour of the meatus may present as an ulcer or mass giving a blood stained otorrhoea and pain. Surgery and radiotherapy will be undertaken.

Although malignancies of the middle ear are rare the most likely to occur are squamous cell carcinomas. They will cause deafness, a blood stained discharge, pain and facial paralysis. Treatment is surgery and radiotherapy.

Care of patients having treatment by radiotherapy

Radiotherapy is used widely in malignant diseases of the head and neck either as:

— primary treatment

— in conjunction with surgery either before or after operation, to help prevent recurrence,

— used palliatively to give relief from symptoms.

Treatment will usually be given using an external beam either with radioactive Cobalt or Linear Accelerator.

Sometimes, however, implants of radioactive needles or seeds incorporated into a dental plate may be used for small tumours with no clinical evidence of spread.

Prior to the commencement of radiotherapy, assessment of the patient is made and any appropriate treatment given.

A full blood count is done and any anaemia corrected as radiation is more effective with a well oxygenated tumour.

Dental treatment is given which in some instances, such as with floor of mouth malignancy, can mean complete dental clearance. Radiotherapy will cause a decreased blood supply to the teeth and increase the risk of osteomyelitis of the mandible.

Radiotherapy near the airway carries the risk of obstruction due to inflammation and oedema. Tracheostomy may, therefore, be performed before treatment commences, when the tissues will heal, in anticipation of possible obstruction.

Any infection such as a chest infection should be treated.

Patients' problems may arise as part of the disease process or as a reaction to treatment.

The nurse must identify actual and potential problems and plan care accordingly.

These problems could be:

dysphagia
dry mouth
loss of the sense of taste
stomatitis
skin reaction
weight loss
hair loss
communication difficulties

either due to voice involvement dry mouth or patient's feeling unable to communicate about the nature of their disease

pain and discomfort
tiredness and lethergy
anxiety and depression.

Special areas to be considered when planning nursing care are covered in the following pages.

Patients' hydration and nutrition

Adequate fluids should be encouraged including high protein drinks. Diet may have to be liquidized and either taken orally or given by tube or total parental nutrition given by sub-clavian line.

Otherwise, a soft nutritional diet is offered taking into consideration patients' preferences. Spicy and acid food fluids should be avoided.

Drugs such as lignocain or steroid swallows may be used to help dysphagia.

Mouth care

Frequent mouth washes should be given, teeth and dentures kept clean. Dentures should be sterilized daily in a suitable fluid and only worn for eating. Loss of secretions encourages secondary infection which must then be treated — for example thrush may be treated with nystatin.

Skin care
Head and neck radiotherapy will almost certainly cause a skin reaction. Any kind of friction should be avoided either from clothes, washing or drying. Water and bland soap can be used and the skin patted dry. Cream soap and talcum containing perfume or zinc must be avoided. Starch baby powder can be used to help drying.

Tracheostomy care
When a tracheostomy has had to be performed the usual care is given but only a plastic tube must be used as metal can interfere with the radiation.

Hair loss
A wig should be provided before it is needed.

Pain and discomfort
Control of pain and discomfort by the effective use of drugs and good nursing care.

Communication
Writing materials and pictures should be available when there is dysphonia. Time should be spent talking to the patients and allowing them to ask questions and express their feelings.

Patient's anxiety
Providing diversions such as television allowing frequent visits. Talking to the patient and giving help and support.

Feeling tired and lethargic
Ensure adequate periods of rest and sleep for the patient.

Social problems
Patients having treatment may be away from work for some time which could mean financial problems. Here the Medical Social Worker will become involved.

When caring for patients with radioactive implants nurses must adhere to the rules regarding safety which apply when nursing patients who are a source of radiation.

Care of patients having Cytotoxic Chemotherapy

Chemotherapy is usually given to try and prevent dissemination of the disease. The aim is to treat microscopic metastases which are not clinically detectable and to halt or slow down the progress of the disease.

It may be given as adjuvant therapy to surgery and radiotherapy and is mainly palliative.

Preparation before treatment will be directed towards treating any infection and ensuring the Hb white cell count and platelets are within normal limits. Prior to each treatment repeat blood counts will be done and the patient's height and weight measured, because drug doses are calculated according to body surface area.

Nurses must be aware of the side effects of the drugs and the actual and potential problems the patient may experience, and plan care accordingly. Possible side effects of the drugs are nausea, vomiting, diarrhoea, stomatitis, hair loss, bone marrow depression causing andemia, leucopenia particularly neutropenia and thrombocytopenia.

Every drug has its own side effects cisplatin, for example, will suppress the bone marrow, is toxic to the kidneys and auditory nerve. Renal functions must be assessed before each treatment and an audiogram done. The patient must be adequately hydrated before and during treatment. Cisplatin can have strong associations with nausea and vomiting but by giving a drug such as Lorazepam the memory of this can be reduced.

The care of the patients receiving chemotherapy will be similar to patients having radiotherapy, as many of the problems they experience will be similar. Care must be planned to include:

— Maintenance of hydration and nutrition.

— Oral care and treatment of any stomatitis.

— Watch for any signs of bleeding e.g. epistaxis, bleeding gums. Care of any transfusions.

— Care of any intravenous infusions and careful observation of the site.

Administration of any drug prescribed such as antiemetics which must be given regularly.

Appropriate care of the patient with diarrhoea which can occur during treatment.

Care of the skin pressure areas.

Prevention of pain and discomfort.

Giving psychological support and care.

Help with any special problems.

Ensure there is a wig available before the patient needs one. With the technique of scalp cooling the loss of hair may now be less.

If the white cell count is low the patient will be nursed in 'protected isolation' to lessen the risk of infection.

A white cell count of less than 2,000 or platelets less than 60,000 means treatment must be stopped until the cell count has improved.

Although student nurses are not directly concerned with the administration of the cytotoxic drugs they should be aware that there are special precautions which must be taken when the drugs are administered.

There should be a safe practice policy for people who are preparing and administering the drugs.

Any extravasation of the drugs can cause tissue necrosis so the site must be closely observed. If extravasation occurs the appropriate treatment for that drug should be promptly given.

A patient may have an anaphylactic reaction when a cytotoxic drug is first administered, therefore supportive measures and drugs must be readily available.

The patient should realize the adverse affects of radiotherapy will last for some time but with chemotherapy they should feel better within about four days.

After both radiotherapy and chemotherapy the care of the patient at home, support of the family and involvement of the social services must be considered and planned.

Patients should return to as normal a life as possible but try to avoid the risk of infection.

It is probably only when caring for patients with malignant disease that the nurse in the ENT area will be called upon, in some instances, to give terminal care.

Then the nursing care must be given to meet the changing needs of the patient, particularly in the areas of pain control, maintaining personal comfort, dignity and giving help and support to the patient and relatives.

Practice Questions

1. What is the role of the speech therapist in the care of the patient who has had a laryngectomy?
2. What is oesophageal speech?
3. List complications of tracheostomy.
4. What advice and help would a patient need before going home after laryngectomy?
5. Mr Peter Jackson, a patient with a glottic carcinoma is admitted for emergency tracheostomy.

   The presenting symptom for this condition will most likely have been

   a cough
   b hoarsness
   c dysphagia
   d feeling a lump

6. He must go straight to theatre so the most important thing for the nurse to do is to
   a shave the neck
   b inform the relatives
   c record the temperature, pulse and blood pressure
   d reassess the patient
7. The hole into the trachea will most likely include
   a 1st tracheal ring
   b 3rd tracheal ring
   c 5th tracheal ring
   d 7th tracheal ring
8. On return to the ward a cuffed tube is in site. The purpose of the cuff is to
   a prevent blood and secretions going down the airway
   b prevent any bleeding
   c prevent the tube being coughed out.
   d in case the patient needs ventilating
9. Mr Jackson will need frequent suction. When performing tracheal suction the sucker should be applied to the catheter
   a intermittently on insertion
   b continually on withdrawal
   c continually on withdrawal and insertion
   d intermittently on withdrawal and insertion
10. The cuffed tube is changed after a few days for a set with a speaking valve. This is called a
    a Negus tube
    b Lombarts tube
    c Jackson tube
    d Pillings tube
11. When comparing the inner and outer tubes of this tracheostomy set, the inner tube should be
    a the same length
    b 2cm longer
    c slightly shorter
    d slightly longer
12. Before he goes home it is important for Mr Jackson to know, that when his tube needs changing
    a he can manage the tube himself
    b the community nurse will change it
    c the GP will change it
    d the hospital staff will change it
13. List the specific areas of care which must be planned when nursing a patient after a commando or composite operation.

14. List the problems a patient may experience who is receiving radiotherapy treatment to the head and neck.
15. Cytotoxic drugs can cause bone marrow depression. What will this result in?
16. What other problems may a patient experience while having treatment with cytotoxic drugs?
17. What nursing measures can be initiated to help with patient with these particular problems?
18. What may be the nursing management of a flap used for reconstruction of a defect?
19. Mr John Smith aged 57 years, a builder, married with three children aged 12, 18 and 20, is admitted for total laryngectomy and block dissection of glands of neck.
    Using a problem solving approach plan Mr Smith's post-operative care and give reasons for this care.

Answers

1. Pre-operative assessment of the patient
   — personality
   — voice
   — background and family.
   Must motivate the patient towards acquiring a new voice.
   Post operatively:
   — when the wound has healed, to teach and help the patient with oesophageal speech
   — alternatively if this is not possible, to provide suitable mechanical equipment for producing speech.
2. Air is swallowed and then regurgitated into the mouth when it is modified into speech by the tongue and lips.
3. Haemorrhage, surgical emphysema, apnoea, crusting, infection, mucosal ulceration, skin excoriation.
   Obstruction from blocked or displaced tube. Lung collapse.
4. Taught care of the stoma.
   Provided with tubes or buttons and should know where to get replacements.
   Advice on suitable clothes.
   Told to avoid if possible, dusty irritation atmospheres and infection.
   To be careful about water.
   How to contact the local laryngectomy club if they wish.
   Who to contact if they have any problems.
5. **b**
6. **d**
7. **b**
8. **a**
9. **b**

10. **a**
11. **d**
12. **a**
13. This will include:
    care of the temporary tracheostomy
    maintaining hydration and nutrition
    intravenous fluids
    naso gastric feeding
    return to normal diet.
    Oral care:
    mouth washes
    gentle swabbing
    gentle irrigation.

    care of wound drainage
    care of any graft and donor sites
    help with any speech difficulties
    psychological support particularly about appearance.
14. Problems related to radiotherapy on head and neck
    — dysphagia
    — dry mouth
    — loss of sense of taste
    — stomatitis
    — skin reaction
    — hair loss
    — tiredness
    — anxiety
    — communication problems.
15. Anaemia
    Thrombocytopenia — risk of bleeding
    Leucopenia — neutropenia — lack of resistance to infection.
16. Problems related to chemotherapy are
    — nausea, vomiting, diarrhoea, stomatitis, hair loss.
17. Regular administration of anti-emetic.
    Adequate fluids.
    Nourishing diet as desired and as able.
    Prompt toilet facilities.
    Personal hygiene.
    Care of the skin and pressure areas.
    Oral hygiene — mouthwashes, care of dentures and teeth.
    Treatment for secondary infection.
    Nystatin for thrush.
    Ensure there is a wig available.
    Appropriate care for any problems related to specific drugs.

18. Management of the flap:
    — no pressure or tension on the graft
    — graft should be pink and warm
    — observe and report it if it becomes cold, mottled, oedematous, inflammed.

    Graft Donor Site
    — this will be covered with split skin
    — covered by dressing e.g. proflavine wool
    — left undisturbed for 7-10 days
    — any unhealed area is cleansed and redressed.

    Split Skin Donor Area
    This will be covered with non adhesive dressing e.g. Tulle gras or meloline held in place by bandages or strapping. After 7-10 days can be soaked off in the bath.

19. CARE PLAN FOR A PATIENT AFTER LARYNGECTOMY

PROBLEMS	CARE	REASONS
Interruption of the normal airway.	Humidification — continuous — gradually wean off.	Prevent crusting.
Depression of cough reflex.	Suction as needed.	Remove secretions.
Cannot easily remove secretions.	Physiotherapy to chest.	
Tracheostomy tube in situ.	Care of tracheostomy tubes.	To maintain airway until stoma healed.
	Cuffed tube — cuff is directed.	Prevent pressure on trachea.
	Change to laryngectomy tube 3-4 days.	
	Change inner — outer tubes as instructed or as needed.	
	Button may be used when tracheostomy stoma has healed.	
	Sutures have been removed.	
Risk of possible post-operative shock — haemorrhage.	Monitor pulse — blood pressure frequently — 4 hourly.	Monitor condition. Observe for any post operative shock — haemorrhage.
	Care of transfusion/infusion.	
	Observation of wound vacuum drainage.	
Wounds.	Observe condition of wounds.	Observe for any signs of inflammation.

PROBLEMS	CARE	REASONS
Neck.	Care of vacuum drainage.	Ensure wound drainage under flaps.
	Remove when drainage is minimal as directed.	
Stoma.	Keep clean — dry. Change dressings. Sutures removed when wounds are healed. Neck — 7-10 days. Stoma — about 10 days.	Prevent infection.
Pharyngeal repair.	Intravenous fluids until tube feed can be given.	Maintain hydration, electrolyte balance.
	Anti-emitics.	Prevent vomiting. Strain on repair.
	Aspirate tube if needed.	
	Record fluid balance.	Monitor fluid balance.
Naso-gastric tube in situ.	Tube feeds introduced day after operation.	Maintain hydration and nutrition.
	Increased to full feed given either continuously by drip or intermittently	
	— Test drink 7-10 days if no leakage	To test pharynx is healed.
	— Oral fluids — Semi solids — Normal diet	Gradual return to normal diet.

PROBLEMS	CARE	REASONS
Can have problems of elimination related to feeding — inactivity — diarrhoea or constipation.	Review method of feeding consult with dietician about feeds.	Prevent loss of fluid nutrients.
	Give medication.	Prevent patient discomfort.
	Observe urinary output. Maintain fluid balance chart.	Monitor fluid balance.
Not able to maintain own hygiene — skin care in the post-operative period.	Help with personal hygiene.	Maintain patients personal hygiene and comfort.
	Care of pressure areas.	
Not taking oral fluid can lead to dry mouth.	Oral care.	Prevent the complication of poor oral hygiene.
Mobility limited to bed area because of equipment.	Encourage leg movements.	Prevent the complications of bad rest.
	Sit out of bed first day gradually ambulate.	
Pain.	Give analgesics which should be drugs which do not depress respiration.	Ensure relief from pain.
Anxiety.	Explain, encourage, reassure.	To help relieve anxiety promote rest.

PROBLEMS	CARE	REASONS
Loss of voice.	Call system to hand.	Maintan communication.
Breakdown of normal communication.	Writing materials.	
Risk of feeling isolated.	Talk to patient.	Prevent isolation.
	Speech therapy when wound is healed.	
May not be able to return to previous work.	Get help from medical social worker.	Lessen difficulties of not being able to return to job.
Different 'body image'.	Plan to work towards rehabilitation.	Enable patient to return to as normal a life as possible.

9 ADVICE FOR EXAMINATION PREPARATION

Start your preparation well in advance of the examination. Make a realistic plan of action that you will be able to achieve.

1. Decide how many hours each day you can set aside for study/revision 2 hours daily × 5 = 10 hours weekly.
2. Make a timetable and slot in all the subjects to be studied. The length of time you allocate depends on the level of difficulty.
3. Study in the same place each day. Sit at a desk or table and have the materials you need at hand, i.e. paper, pencils, crayons, text books, lecture notes and a rubber. Write in pencil so that mistakes or unwanted notes can be erased (paper is expensive).
4. You must work at concentrating on your task, don't allow yourself to think of anything else so that you waste time.
5. If you are tired or upset, relax before attempting to settle.
6. Work at each of the goals you have set yourself as widely as you can.
7. Reward yourself when a goal is achieved so that you associate pleasure with studying.
8. Success is not a matter of luck but of good planning and self-discipline.
9. Learning is an active process so:
   a Study using a logical approach. Sequence the material and go from easy to more difficult concepts.
   b Don't try to learn chunks of material, skim the passage and try to understand. Underline key words or sentences. Use a dictionary.
   c Overlearn material and consciously recall and reinforce your memory. Commit your thoughts to paper.
   d Use mnemonics as a memory aid.
   e Ask yourself questions, apply the material, compare with management of actual patients you have nursed. Have discussions with friends/tutors.
   f Ask your tutors for help if you do not understand the relevance of a topic.
   g Learn to draw and label line drawings correctly.
   h Test yourself using past examination questions.
   i Get your relations or friends to ask you questions.
10. Cultivate a fast reading style. Use several textbooks with your notes. Make your own notes when you have analysed the meaning of a passage. Begin to read with a question in mind and ask yourself questions when you have read a paragraph/chapter. Read quickly then re-read.
11. What you want to achieve is efficiency of study with economy of effort.

Examination technique

1. Listen to the invigilator's instructions and follow them carefully. Have your number card signed and available for inspection. Be prepared with pens, pencils, a rubber and ruler.
2. Read the instructions on the front cover of the book and comply with them, i.e. start a question on a fresh page, number your questions carefully, write legibly. Note how many questions are to be attempted, how much time is allowed etc.
3. Objective type questions test a wide area of knowledge, recognition and recall in a short time. Consider the questions carefully, and choose what you believe to be the correct answer from the distractors, do not just guess.
4. Essay questions test:
   a Knowledge
   b Comprehension
   c Application
   d Communication
   e Synthesis.
5. Read all the questions carefully on both sides of the paper, identify all parts of the question.
   a Don't be concerned that others have started to write.
   b Select the questions you feel most able to answer.
   c Tick your selection in order of sequence.
   d Analyse the setting of the question. Is the scene in hospital or the community? What is the importance of age, sex, marital/social status, environment, psychological well-being, needs of the patient in the examiner's mind.
   Underline these points and develop them.
   e Note the essential points that have to be made in your answer in the margin of the paper.
   f Pay attention to the weighting of each part of the question, these should help you plan the time to be spent on each part.
   g Ten minutes spent in planning is the most effective way of using the examination time.
   h When you start to write:
   (i) answer the parts in order of a, b, c, d.
   (ii) write legibly, be logical (first things first)
   (iii) concentrate on the main parts, don't waffle and repeat yourself.
   (iv) if a diagram is asked for make a clear line drawing and label it clearly.
   (v) leave time at the end for reading your answers.

Remember that a good essay has an introduction, a development and a conclusion, and should be clear and concise.

NOTES

NOTES

NOTES

NOTES

NOTES

NOTES

NOTES

NOTES

NOTES